TRUE BLUE

Blue walked into the living room and found Toni sitting on the couch. "You didn't want to stay outside?"

She rubbed her arms. "It was getting a bit chilly out there. I brought in the champagne so we could have another toast."

He started to move past her. "First let me make sure all the candles are put out—"

She grabbed his arm and tugged him down beside her. "I turned out all the lights. Blew out the candles. I put the cake away. Everything has been done. Relax."

He let her urge him back against the sofa cushions and push a glass of champagne into his hand. She curled against his side, looking down at him. He sighed, feeling that familiar rush that came with her closeness. "Okay, what are we toasting?"

She wet her lips slowly, raising her glass. "To fulfilling dreams and living out fantasies." She touched her glass to his and took a sip.

Blue had barely taken a swallow of champagne before Toni was lifting the glass from his hand and setting it on the table. Warning bells went off in his head. He could see where this was headed, and if he allowed himself to start kissing Toni he wasn't sure he'd be able to stop.

BOOK YOUR PLACE ON OUR WEBSITE AND MAKE THE ARABESQUE ROMANCE CONNECTION!

We've created a customized website just for our very special Arabesque readers, where you can get the inside scoop on everything that's going on with Arabesque romance novels.

When you come online, you'll have the exciting opportunity to:

- View covers of upcoming books

- Learn about our future publishing schedule (listed by publication month and author)

- Find out when your favorite authors will be visiting a city near you.
- Search for and order backlist books from our line catalog

- Check out author bios and background information

- Send e-mail to your favorite authors

- Join us in weekly chats with authors, readers and other guests

- Get writing guidelines

- AND MUCH MORE!

Visit our website at
http://www.arabesquebooks.com

TRUE BLUE

ROBYN AMOS

BET Publications, LLC
www.msbet.com
www.arabesquebooks.com

ARABESQUE BOOKS are published by

BET Publications, LLC
c/o BET BOOKS
One BET Plaza
1900 W Place NE
Washington, D.C. 20018-1211

BET Books is a trademark of Black Entertainment Television, Inc. Arabesque, the Arabesque logo and the BET Books logo are Reg. U.S. Pat. & TM Off.

First Printing: February, 1999
10 9 8 7 6 5 4 3 2 1

Printed in the United States of America

*This book is dedicated to Michele Thomas—
a true blue sister and friend.*

Special thanks to Barbara Cummings, Judy Fitzwater,
Pat Gagne, Ann Kline, Vicki Singer and
Karen Smith, who have always been there for me
when I've needed them.

PROLOGUE

"What the hell do you mean, she moved?" JB stared through the glass partition at his younger twin brothers, better known as Tweedle Dumb and Tweedle Dumber.

Barry—Tweedle–Dumb, shrugged, rubbing the back of his neck. For his visit to prison he wore a black *America's Most Wanted* T-shirt, sporting large iron bars. "We did what you said, JB, but when we rolled up in there her place was empty."

"But Barry and I analyticalized the situation very carefully," Larry cut in. He'd dressed more subtly, in a denim work shirt with bold black prison numbers printed on the back and chest. "We were able to find out where she went."

JB rubbed his temple warily. What should have been a simple mission had grown complicated. With his brothers involved, that could only mean trouble. "And how did you do that?"

"We asked the landlady." Larry's lips formed his standard vacant grin. "At first she wanted to know why we wanted to know. I told her that this girl has property that belongs to us."

JB didn't bother reprimanding them. It would only fall on deaf ears. Barry and Larry had received the family good looks. All three brothers shared a strong family resemblance. But the twins—barely over twenty-one with smooth faces and guileless smiles—had the perfect looks for running cons.

Unfortunately, they shared only one brain between them.

"Don't you want to know where she went, JB?" Barry arched one eyebrow and grinned, clearly proud to have made the discovery. "Your girl skipped off to Florida."

Dropping his forehead into the palm of his hand, JB closed his eyes. His life had been going downhill lately, and the hill was getting steeper every day. The fact that he was sitting in jail waiting to be prosecuted for cons he'd committed dating back to his teens was the least of his worries. He hadn't bothered trying to make bail just yet. Everything had to be in place first. Once he got out, JB had no intention of going back.

Right now his biggest problem was that his future happiness depended upon the two biggest idiots in the world. JB ran his first con when he was eight-years-old. Since then he'd cultivated plenty of connections, but each of those resources came with prices attached. At least when he got his brothers to recover his money, he could disappear without sharing a penny. They weren't clever enough to screw him on the deal.

Bearing that in mind, JB pressed on, forcing himself to remain patient with his dim-witted siblings. "Okay, so we've established that my ex-girlfriend is now in Florida. I still need to get those bonds."

Barry and Larry shrugged in unison. "We got your back."

JB pretended to think it over carefully. "Well, it looks like you're going to have to go to Florida, boys." He looked down at his regulation prison issue uniform. "I'm not exactly in any position to travel right now."

Barry nodded gravely. "But JB, we don't even know where she is in Florida."

"Don't worry. You leave that up to me. I'll handle all the arrangements. You two just go home and prepare for a little trip."

Larry's eyes lit up. "Really? Where are we going?"

Barry punched him in the arm. "Florida, dummy."

Larry scowled, looking hurt. "I knew that. I was just joking."

After his brothers left, a prison guard led JB back to his cell. He hadn't counted on Antoinette Rivers picking up and moving to Florida, but that was just a minor setback, like his incarceration. All he had to do was hang tight a while longer, and everything would fall back into place. He was like a cat—he had nine lives, and he always landed on his feet.

CHAPTER ONE

The dance floor of Blue Paradise nightclub was packed with energetic bodies. The crowd was partying as if it was 1999. And that was because it was—and had been ever since the club rang in the new year, less than an hour ago.

From his private office above, Blue Cooper gazed at the club scene with distant eyes. The song "1999", recorded by The Artist Formerly Known As Prince, vibrated from every speaker in the building. It didn't take a genius to know that it would become the club's most requested song in the coming year.

Through two-way mirrored glass, Blue watched couples gyrate and twist under colorful, rotating lights. His sense of isolation grew. At that moment, even sipping his all-time favorite chocolate drink, Yoo-hoo, gave him little comfort. Instead, Blue felt his mood shrinking into the black shadows at the back of his mind.

He wasn't sure why, because his life wasn't dissatisfying. Blue Paradise was one of the most popular nightclubs in West Palm Beach. And, when Blue couldn't be found at the apex of Florida nightlife he kept busy. Whenever his friends hit a snag, Blue was always the first man called.

They knew they could count on him because he was "true blue". That was his motto, and it was more than just a catchy phrase to replace *hello* when he answered the phone. It was the way he lived his life.

He didn't mind running off at a moment's notice to help a friend in need, but he was thirty-two-years-old and the only thing he had to look forward to was his next excursion. He found himself prolonging his adventures to put off the inevitable chill that came each time he tried to sink back into his life.

Blue turned his back to the window and crossed the room to his desk. He tried not to spend his nights at the club alone in his office. The room had a full lounge area and bar where he could entertain his guests privately, but Blue rarely used it. He preferred to mingle with the crowd and interact with his staff.

He needed people. If he spent too much time alone he couldn't tame the savage memories of the places he'd been, and things he'd seen, in his past. He needed to keep them caged in darkness, where they couldn't claw at his heart and tear at his sanity.

Yet he found himself alone more frequently. He could feel himself changing. It didn't take long for his dark thoughts to become unchained. It was a struggle not to succumb to his bitter moods.

He wasn't the brooding type, but that was by careful design. He'd seen what happened when emotions went numb. His best friend, Jax, had been a prime example. For all the years Blue had known Jax the man had remained cold and stoic, completely expressionless—

until he met a sprite-like ball of fire named Coco who had melted the wall of ice Jax had built around his heart. Jax had been one of the lucky ones. But Blue had seen many others who hadn't recovered from the harsh hands life had dealt them.

That was why Blue didn't drink anything stronger than a Yoo-hoo or take part in anything that would make him more vulnerable to the demons he kept shackled in his head. That was why he lived his life as honestly as his past would allow.

Despite the urge to stay isolated from those who couldn't possibly understand him, Blue forced himself down the winding stairs and through the corridor that led to the club's main room.

The throng instantly welcomed him. Regulars knew him by name and turned to greet him or slap him on the back as he made his way through the crowd. He got along well with his staff because he made an effort to pitch in, or make mischief, wherever he could.

Some nights he poured drinks at the bar, checked coats in the cloakroom, or pitched drunkards alongside the bouncers. On a good night he'd head for the deejay booth and they'd let him spin a few hits. Most often they'd hand him a microphone to pump up the crowd.

Blue would laugh and joke with the fellas, flirt with the ladies, and maybe even go out onto the floor for a dance or two. Everyone admired Blue's easy charm and natural wit. They had no idea his jocularity was a vital weapon in the daily battle for his soul.

"Hey, Rutherford!" Blue climbed to the top of the security balcony on the other end of the club and slapped hands with a broad bouncer with a crew cut.

"Blue, my man! Happy New Year, buddy!"

Blue leaned against the rail. "You too, man. How was Vegas? Did you win big bucks?"

"Nah, Shirl wouldn't let me near the blackjack tables. She made me promise to give up gambling as my New Year's resolution." Rutherford folded his massive arms and faced Blue. "You bother with that stuff? Resolutions?"

"No, I got out of that habit a long time ago." Resolutions had been hard to make when he wasn't even sure if he'd be around to see the new year through.

But those days were past. By the old standards, his life had calmed down considerably. He wasn't getting any younger, and the old rules no longer applied. It was time for him to make some changes in his life.

Blue watched the crowd below throb as the deejay cranked up the tempo and turned on the smoke machine. "This year I might make an exception, though."

"Yeah? What's your resolution?"

"It may be time for me to start thinking about settling down." Blue felt his skin heat. He hadn't known he was going to say that until the words tumbled from his mouth. But now that he'd said them out loud, he knew they were true. "A wife. Family. The whole nine yards."

A wide grin split the younger man's face. "Really? Got anybody in mind?"

"Nope. That's the problem." Blue shook his head, giving him a conspiratorial look. He often found himself talking to Rutherford because of the man's cool, even temperament. He wasn't a macho hothead like many of the bouncers who worked at Blue Paradise. "Just between you and me? I can't remember the last time I went out on an actual date."

Rutherford made a face. "Now I know you're pulling my leg. I've seen how the women around here crawl all over you. Put out the word that you're interested, and they'll be lined up around the block."

Blue knew that to the untrained eye he appeared to be a regular lady-killer. He was frequently accused of being West Palm Beach's very own Don Juan, but it was all an illusion. He knew how to turn up the charm and flirt without letting anyone get close. The fact was, he'd always been a one woman man.

Rutherford eyed him skeptically. "I can't believe this. You're really thinking about taking yourself off the market?"

"Yeah." Blue grinned. "If I can find a good woman like Shirl."

"No, you don't want a woman like Shirl. She's too difficult. You need a woman who knows how to have a good time." He studied the dance floor. "Like that one in red over there."

Blue followed the bouncer's pointing finger to a petite woman wearing a skintight, red catsuit. She had a short, spiky haircut and was pelvic-thrusting atop one of the platforms. He threw his head back and laughed, then slapped Rutherford on the back. "No way, man. She's not my type."

"No? Then who is?" He gestured around the room. "Take your pick."

Blue didn't bother looking. "No. She's not here. I'm not interested in a nightclub groupie. I'll know her when I see her."

Rutherford snorted. "That's bull. I've been married for five years, and I can tell you, man, it doesn't work like that."

Blue flicked his finger at his friend's noggin. "That's because you're a meathead, Rutherford. You were lucky to find a woman who was willing to put up with you." The bouncer laughed, and Blue continued more seriously. "Actually, I have a keen sense of timing. I always have, and something tells me . . . it's about that time."

"For what?"

"For me to meet *the one.*"

"Don't tell me you actually buy into all that soulmate crap."

For the second time that night Blue's friend Jax came to mind. He'd seen that man undergo a complete transformation, and all because of a woman. Like David with Goliath, Coco had felled a mighty giant with the most basic of weapons.

Blue's eyelids drifted shut for a moment as he considered Rutherford's question. Then he opened them, seeing the world more clearly than he had for quite some time.

"Yeah. I know it sounds corny, but I do . . . and my instincts never fail me."

Whenever Antoinette Rivers thought she'd gotten a firm grip on life, things spun out of control.

One minute she was safe on even ground, the next she was screaming for dear life. "April! Help me, April!"

The pavement sloped unexpectedly, and she found herself staring at a steep set of steps. The in-line skates strapped to her feet became shackles, gripping her ankles as they propelled her toward certain death.

Her sister was already far ahead, skating effortlessly through the winding maze of wrought-iron tables that waited at the bottom of the steps.

Undiluted terror coursed through Toni's veins as she realized the horrible truth. "I don't know how to stop! April!"

Following her sister's lead, she veered toward the handicap ramp. The skates went from zero to sixty in two seconds flat, and Toni raced down the ramp like a runaway train.

April finally turned around and saw that her sister was out of control. "You'll be fine. 'En 'ou get to the 'ottom of the hill, uurp ound!"

Wind rushed in her ears. "Whaaaaat?"

April was making a circular motion with her hands. Toni held her breath and concentrated on maintaining her balance. It wasn't difficult to imagine herself sliding across the concrete on her stomach.

"Look out!" Toni yelled at the couple carrying open drinks across her path. "Comin' through!" When she finally leveled out, she was going faster than ever.

April continued to make air traffic control signals with her hands, but Toni sped right past her, picking up momentum. The terror gripping her heart intensified. She saw no hope of slowing down.

Was that a lake up ahead?

Frantic at the thought of becoming fish bait, Toni began turning her body in a wide arc. She curved off the path into grass and came to a dead stop. Suddenly, she was pitching head first toward a double-sided park bench. Afraid of head-butting the man sitting on the other side, she managed to spin around and land on the bench properly, if not comfortably.

Toni clutched her heart. Was twenty-eight too young to have cardiac arrest?

"Are you all right?" asked a deep male voice from the opposite side of the bench.

With an embarrassed nod, Toni slid down on the seat, refusing to look up.

"She's fine. She's fine." April expertly whooshed to a stop in front of Toni, then flopped down beside her.

By the time Toni mustered the nerve to peek over her shoulder, the man had already returned his attention to the laptop computer in front of him.

Toni dragged air into her heaving lungs, still shaking

from her brush with death. "You could have killed me, April."

Her sister fanned herself with her hand. "What are you talking about?" She pulled her hair up off her neck and tilted her face toward the sun as if she were lying on the beach.

"You know exactly what I'm talking about. You said Florida was the perfect place to learn in-line skating. All flat land. You could have warned me about the steps!" Toni noted the slightly hysterical edge to her voice.

Her sister blinked innocently. "I'm sorry. I forgot." Then she nudged her with her shoulder. "Besides, wasn't it exhilarating? What an adventure."

Toni wasn't listening. "And why didn't you tell me how to stop these things? I think that's essential information. How did you know I wouldn't accidentally roll into traffic, or into a lake, or . . . or off a cliff?"

"Lighten up, Toni," April said casually. "There aren't any cliffs around here. Besides, you're fine."

"No thanks to you." Toni glared at her.

The man on the bench chuckled behind them. Both women looked over at him and the laughter turned into throat clearing.

Toni turned back around, folding her arms over her chest. She wasn't going to forgive April for this. "I should have left you in D.C. We've been down here for two months, and already you're trying to kill me for my share of the money."

"That's silly, Toni. If that's true, why did I give you the money in the first place?" April picked at her chipping, purple nail polish.

"Because you didn't know you'd given me a winning lottery ticket. If you had, you probably would have kept it for yourself."

"Mumble, grumble." April feigned a hurt expression. "How can you think so little of your baby sister?"

Toni sighed. Her sister could be thoughtless, but she was also incredibly supportive at the most unexpected times. Besides, Toni could only blame herself for this particular misadventure. She shouldn't have let April talk her into in-line skating in the first place.

She bent forward and began unleashing her feet. "I'm taking these things off. I don't care if I have to walk all the way back to the car in my socks."

"I can't believe you're giving up already. You promised to try to have a little fun."

Toni narrowed her eyes at April. "I told you that we could take a couple weeks off to enjoy Florida after we got the coffee shop in place. I did not say that you could strap wheels to my feet and roll me off the face of the earth."

April stared at the skates Toni had stacked beside her. "You paid almost two hundred dollars for those skates. You're going to have to wear them again."

Toni pursed her lips. April knew she was a stickler about getting her money's worth. "Of course I'll wear them again, but not until I begin classes taught by a *qualified* instructor."

"Come on, when are we going to really start enjoying the money? Ever since we got it, you've been spending it on practical things like setting up the business and moving us into a condo. When are we going to buy a couple of flashy cars, or throw a wild party? So far the most frivolous thing you've done is buy a new wardrobe."

Now that they actually had money, Toni was concerned that they not blow it. "We moved to a warmer climate. A new wardrobe was practical."

Toni felt a grin touch her lips. There was nothing

practical about the rich silks and colorful fabrics that
made up the sexy sarongs, sundresses and elegant shorts
sets she'd bought. But Toni was proud of herself. She
hadn't let April talk her into a dramatic makeover. The
clothes were in keeping with her natural style, with just
a *hint* more sensuality.

"How many times do I have to explain this, April?
Money doesn't go as far as it used to. We're going to
have to be careful with it if we don't want to end up
deeper in the hole than when we started."

"Yadda yadda yadda."

Toni found herself becoming exasperated with April,
as she often did. Her sister wasn't stupid, but she
believed in living for the moment and worrying about
the future later.

Physically, the sisters looked a lot alike. They had
similar long, brown curls, though Toni kept hers neatly
subdued with clips, hairbands, combs, or ribbons
instead of letting them spring vibrantly around her face
as April did. They also shared the same golden skin,
wide, sienna eyes and full, pouty lips. Their taste in
clothing was the main thing that really set them apart.
April loved sexy clothes that were flashy and colorful.
Toni preferred more classic, sophisticated styles.

"April, you're only four years younger than I am.
When are you going to grow up? Running a small busi-
ness is risky. We could lose our entire investment if we
don't make smart decisions. Coffee.com has to come
first."

April shifted into a sexy pose, showing off her skin-
tight shorts and halter top as two good-looking men
walked by.

"We're the same people, with or without wealth,"
Toni continued. "Money comes and goes, and we have
to be prepared for the worst." Toni tugged at the over-

sized T-shirt that was knotted at the hip of her spandex shorts. "Are you listening to me?"

"Of course." April's gaze was still following the two young studs. She lifted her hand to wave when one of them winked at her.

"You don't have to be so flirtatious," Toni said, shoving April's arm.

"I'm just being friendly." Her sister shrugged. "Besides, just because you're feeling bitter about men doesn't mean I have to agree. We're in West Palm Beach. Tight buns and hard muscles everywhere you look. I'd hate to see you turn your back on men just because one lousy creep—"

Toni rolled her eyes. "It wasn't just one lousy creep. Jordan was just the *last* lousy creep . . . and the worst."

Involuntarily, she winced. Her shelves had once been crammed with books like *How to Love a Black Man, 101 Tips for a Healthy Relationship,* and *A Woman's Guide to Love and Marriage,* and still her love life had been one disaster after another. Her relationship with Jordan Banks had put her other romantic failures to shame.

Her cheeks still stung with humiliation every time she remembered walking into that Washington, D.C. police station several months ago. It was bad enough that she'd arrived expecting to bail her boyfriend out for having one too many drinks and then attempting to drive home, but Toni'd never dreamed she'd discover Jordan was a con artist with multiple aliases and a record dating back to his teens.

That's why he hadn't called her to bail him out. He'd called their mutual friend, Alex, who had been previously occupied at one o'clock that Saturday morning. He'd passed the urgent message for bail money on to Toni. She didn't know who was more shocked that morning, Jordan, when he saw *her* instead of Alex, or her, when she found out her boyfriend of six months was a criminal.

"I noticed you didn't bring any of your self-help relationship books with us. I don't think that's a good sign," April said.

"I gave most of them to The Salvation Army. I'm through with pop psychology. I've probably read every piece of relationship advice from early Dr. Ruth to last month's 'Keeping Your Man' edition of *Cosmopolitan*. Look where it's gotten me."

April shook her head in disbelief. "I can't believe you gave away all those books. You had enough to start your own library."

"I've finally realized that books aren't the answer. I bet you didn't even read the one I lent *you*. The one about going from one-night stands to the love of a lifetime in just six easy steps."

April began dusting off her skates. "I flipped through it."

"Yes, but did you *read* it?"

"I picked up a few things that were useful."

Toni shook her head. "Clearly, you haven't put any of them into practice. When was the last time you had a relationship that lasted more than two weeks?"

"What was the point in building attachments right before moving away? I'll settle down now that we're in Florida."

Toni gave her a skeptical look.

"You never answered my question," April said, changing the subject. "Are you just giving up on the advice, or are you giving up men altogether?"

"I'm not giving up. I'm just taking a break."

Toni had given that particular issue a lot of thought after her last bad break up. What she needed was a change of pace. For a woman who had always prided herself on being practical and responsible, she'd been tossing around some pretty radical ideas. She wasn't quite sure if she had the courage to go through with what she had in mind, but just thinking about it gave her a little thrill.

"I know exactly what you need." April looked at her with a wicked smile, stood, and did a spin in front of Toni. "I'm still in charge of entertainment, and there's supposed to be a really hot club about two blocks from here. I want to go there tonight."

Toni shook her head, not wanting to move, let alone think about clubbing. "I don't think so, April. Yesterday we swam with the dolphins, and last week we hit Disney World. I wouldn't mind staying in tonight."

April spun around again. "Either we go clubbing tonight or you buy me a Jaguar."

Toni laughed. "I will not be blackmailed. I'm staying in tonight. You can go by yourself."

Her sister started up the hill. "Forest green with creamy white leather interior."

Toni stood and stared after her. "Give it up. I'm not changing my mind."

April continued forward, calling over her shoulder, "And tinted windows."

Toni found herself bounding up the hill, clutching her skates to her chest. "April! I'm not going to let you do this." She ran to catch up as her sister disappeared over the top of the hill. "April!"

It was all about timing, and as usual Blue's was impeccable. He closed his laptop and laughed. Sometimes life's most important moments boiled down to being in the right place at the right time.

He'd just decided he was ready for a serious relationship, and a perfect candidate walked right into his life. Well, she hadn't exactly walked. Rather, she'd streaked into his life like a bat out of hell with her hair on fire.

He'd blatantly eavesdropped on Toni's conversation with her sister, and he wasn't the least bit ashamed. In addition to being highly amusing, their conversation told him everything he needed to know in just a few minutes.

That woman definitely intrigued him. Though he hadn't gotten a good look at her from where he sat, he couldn't miss the beautiful, long, brown curls spilling from her ponytail. Her voice was low and sexy, and she spoke in a clear, cultured tone.

Her sister came across as carefree and witty, but Blue found Toni's stability and practicality more appealing. Party girls were a dime a dozen at the club. It was rare to find a woman who could carry on a real conversation.

Blue grinned to himself as he remembered the mini lectures Toni had lobbed at her younger sister. She had all the outward appearances of what he wanted. At this stage, it was difficult to tell just how conservative she was. His grin became wicked. Even if she were downright prudish, Blue wouldn't mind. It was always fun to awaken a woman's more primitive sensual appetites for the first time.

He wanted the whole white picket fence package. Blue knew he was putting a lot of weight on one conversation, but there were certain times in his life when things simply clicked into place. Toni had a spark and a feistiness that assured him he'd never be bored.

Blue sighed at his good fortune. He didn't even have to worry about when he'd see her again. From the looks of things, it was more than likely that April would win this particular disagreement. Toni was going to find herself clubbing that night, whether she wanted to or not.

Lucky for Blue, the hottest club in West Palm Beach, let alone in the next two blocks, was Blue Paradise.

CHAPTER TWO

April Rivers stood on the deck outside Blue Paradise, admiring the biceps on the man beside her. A quiet sigh escaped her lips. She was about to give away yet another hot prospect. She couldn't wait to find Toni a man so that she could concentrate on her own social life. So many men, so little time.

Oops! She was backsliding. Toni was the one who needed to have an affair. *She* was supposed to be looking for a deep, *meaningful* relationship. April almost laughed. Did such a thing exist?

"No, I'm not kidding," she said to the sexy body-builder. "My sister's latest book was hotter than the *Kama Sutra*."

She watched Jerry—Jermaine, or whatever he'd said his name was—grin lustfully. "Really?" His dark eyes glittered with eagerness.

"Yes, but if you meet her, play it cool. She's very modest. Toni doesn't like guys hitting on her just because she writes erotica." April downed the last swallow of her drink, watching him shift from foot to foot.

"Sure, sure. I understand." He scanned the outdoor bar area, flexing his hands with impatience. "Where is she?"

"The ladies' room. She'll be out soon." April tried not to giggle. These guys were eating this stuff up.

She and Toni walked into the club almost two hours ago. Toni had spent the first hour sitting at their table like a cardboard cutout. She had little interest in their surroundings—especially the decorative *male* furnishings.

Just as April had expected, Toni wasn't giving the place a chance. Fortunately, April knew a few tricks that would help her sister ease into the nightlife. A few choice words whispered in the right ears, and Toni spent the second hour on the dance floor. So what if April told a few fibs to get the ball rolling? Maybe Toni *would* take up belly dancing in the near future.

Toni stepped onto the deck and April waved her over. "Here she comes."

"Finally, some breathing room." Toni pushed her hair off her shoulders. "It's so packed inside I'm surprised more people aren't crowding out here for air."

"There's another deck with a dance floor on the other side." April turned to the bodybuilder, who was leering at Toni. She fought back the urge to jab him in the ribs. It would help if he wasn't so obvious. Sooner or later Toni was going to catch on, but with any luck it would be too late by then. "Toni this is—"

"Jeremy," the man supplied, reaching out to swallow Toni's hand with his.

Toni smiled politely. "Nice to meet you."

April grinned, twirling her empty glass. "I'm heading for the bar."

Toni turned around to follow her. "That sounds like a good—"

"No, you stay here and keep Jeremiah company. I'll bring something back for you." April slipped away before Toni could protest. She chuckled to herself. "I'm such a good sister."

This was the one night Blue didn't want to be stuck behind the bar serving drinks. Unfortunately, his bartender, Paolo was going to be a couple of hours late.

"There you go, ladies. Enjoy." Blue placed drinks in front of two attractive young women. He had started to turn away when one of them grabbed his wrist.

"Wait. Why don't you stay and chat a while?" She gazed at him through her eyelashes. "It's not busy yet."

Blue smiled and gently removed her hand, giving it a gentle pat as he laid it back on the bar. "Sorry, sweetheart, but if I don't look busy the boss might fire me." He gave her a wink and backed away, ignoring her sexy pout.

Old habits die hard. Picking up a rag Blue wiped down the bar, then rearranged the cocktail napkins. He hadn't forgotten his resolve to start dating again, yet he continued to sidestep every flirtatious comment and "come hither" look he received. Now he couldn't seem to muster enough enthusiasm to set the ball in motion— not since that afternoon in the park.

Blue knew it was ridiculous to pin his hopes on a girl—especially one he'd never seen face to face—just because of a conversation he'd overheard. But his instincts never failed him. If nothing else, the situation was worth investigating. That was, if Toni showed up tonight. And if she did, would he escape bar duty in time to find her?

"I'd like a piña colada, please?"

Blue turned around and paused, taking a long look at the woman in front of him. Was that . . . ? No, it wasn't possible to conjure people with the power of thought—but luck was another matter. That had to be the sister, April.

She wore a black, tropical print halter top with a matching mini skirt, and her hair spilled like a waterfall from a giant ponytail on top of her head. Blue had an eye for detail, and these details didn't belong to Toni.

He placed a napkin in front of her and picked up a cocktail glass. "Can I interest you in a Blue Lagoon? It's a Blue Paradise special. Like a piña colada, only better."

April leaned against the bar. "Let me guess—it's blue?"

"You got it."

"Just like your eyes." She gave him a long, hard stare. "Honey, you've got some gorgeous eyes."

"You're too kind." Blue gave her a bashful grin. "What will it be?"

"One Blue Lagoon." She looked over her shoulder, shaking her head. "No, two. No . . . you'd better make that one."

Blue stopped reaching for glasses and gave her a sly smile. "What's the matter? Your imaginary friend can't make up his mind?"

April didn't miss a beat. "No, he's easy. Straight Tequila. But he's home sick tonight. I can't decide whether or not to get my sister a drink. Make it one. Some things she's got to . . . see for herself."

Blue looked past April and saw Toni standing across the deck. She was talking to a guy best described as a giant muscle. "She's here."

"What?"

"Uh, that's your sister? Over there?" Her hair was parted so that her soft curls fell primarily over the left side of her face. Even from a distance he could see she had lovely features.

April followed his gaze. "Yep, that's her." As she turned back to face him Blue didn't miss the calculating expression that flashed across her face. "I had to drag her out of the house tonight. She's been working hard all week."

Blue realized she was leading him, so he asked the expected question. "Really? What does she do?" He remembered something about a coffee shop.

"We just opened an aromatherapy massage salon." Her gaze raked him up and down like an antique dealer studying a piece for flaws. "My sister is an expert in the exotic art of Chinese oil rubs."

"How intriguing," he said, trying not to show his confusion. Either that was a blatant lie, or he needed a refresher course in the difference between coffee and massage oil.

April nodded. "It's very impressive. Toni's one of only eight people in this country who knows the ritual, but she's the modest type. That's why, if you meet her, you probably shouldn't mention it."

"Of course not." Blue nodded, placing her drink on the bar. "I can see why she wouldn't want anyone to get the wrong idea." What was this girl up to?

"Exactly." April grinned, glancing over her shoulder. "Uh oh!"

Blue raised his gaze and saw that Toni seemed upset with Muscle Man. What appeared to be a look of shock quickly heated to anger. He couldn't hear what they were saying, but he could see harsh words being exchanged.

April grabbed her drink and pushed away from the

bar. "I'd better get over there and referee." It was already too late. Just as she turned around, Toni's hand cracked hard against Muscle Man's cheek. "Oops! Looks like Jericho couldn't keep his mouth shut, after all."

Blue watched April hurry across the deck toward Toni. He was beginning to get a clear picture of just what was going on. He settled back to watch the fireworks.

April strikes again! Toni said to herself as she marched toward her sister, visions of homicide dancing in her head.

April met her halfway. "What's the problem, Sis? Looks as if you and Jedidiah aren't getting along."

"His name's Jeremy, and no, we didn't get along. He asked me if he could help with my research. Naturally, I asked, what research?" Toni paused to see if April had guessed where this was going.

Her expression remained carefully blank. "What?"

"All I'm going to say is that it involved an all-night laundromat and some positions I've never heard of."

"Really? I'm shocked." April tried to fake it, but her lips began to quiver until a sly grin curved its way out.

"You should be. *Somehow* he got the impression that I write erotica." Toni ignored the fact that she'd just piqued the interest of two men standing nearby. She tilted her head to one side. "Hmm, now where would he have gotten an idea like that?" She glared at April.

"Strange." April quickly lifted her drink to her lips. "Mmm, this is great. You should try this."

"Does this have anything to do with that guy you introduced me to earlier? He asked me if I wanted to paint him. I thought it was a misunderstanding. Especially when he said that *he* wanted to be the canvas."

"Ooh, that could be interesting." April clearly couldn't control herself one minute longer. A volcano of giggles erupted from her lips. "Why don't you have a Blue Lagoon and think it over? The bartender's that way."

Toni felt like shaking her. How could she be so casual about this? "It's all starting to make sense. All those men who've been ogling me all night. I should have known you had something to do with it." Toni crossed her arms and gave her little sister an I-Mean-Business look. "What's going on, April? Tell me. Now."

"All right." With a resigned sigh, April shuffled her platform sandals, which made her three inches taller than Toni's five-foot, six inches. "Okay. I confess. I *may* have given a few people the wrong impression tonight."

"Keep talking."

"A few guys may think that you're into something slightly more exotic than coffee. But before you get mad, I want you to know that I was only trying to help. When we first came in you weren't mingling. I was helping you break the ice."

Toni dragged a hand through her hair. "What have you been telling them?"

"It's not as bad as you think. Let's see . . . I told Jerome over there that you write erotic novels. I told the guy from Miami that you were a belly dancer. Um, then there was the—"

"Stop right there. I don't want to hear any more." Toni threw up her hands. "What were you thinking?"

"Why are you so uptight? I was very selective. I should have known you would take this the wrong way." April gave her a pouting look. "I just wanted you to have a good time. Shoot me for putting your happiness before my own. I haven't danced once tonight because of you."

Toni rolled her eyes. There was no reasoning with

April sometimes. The only reason she'd received so much attention was that April had been making up wild stories about her. For *this* she was supposed to be grateful?

"Look, just promise me that you'll stop it, okay? I know you thought you were helping me, but I don't need that kind of help."

April shrugged. "Fine. Go get yourself a drink and try to relax." She nudged Toni toward the bar. "They're playing my song. I'm going to go dance."

Toni rubbed her temples. At this point she *could* use a drink. Suddenly her whole body was wound tighter than a corkscrew. She'd probably be dodging sex-crazed men for the rest of the night. She stared after April, wondering how her sister managed to do this to her every time.

Toni was no longer accepting outside advice about her love life. She wasn't even sure if she wanted one right now, but if she did make that decision it wouldn't be the way it had been in the past. No more broken hearts. No more disappointments. No more Mr. Nice Guy/Boy Next Door types who turned out to be lowlifes.

Part of her wondered what it would be like to date a real bad boy for a change. Why not have a passionate fling for once? This time *she* could call all the shots.

Toni laughed to herself. She had no idea if she could pull it off—it was difficult not to think in terms of forever. She wasn't in the mood to be let down again, though. Besides, every woman deserved one smoldering old flame to remember fondly after she's settled down in the world of marriage and family.

Walking up to the bar, Toni sat on a stool. There were two bartenders working behind the bar, and they were both busy filling orders. The one closest to her had his hands full with a bold female customer. "Hey sexy, can I get a Blueberry wine?"

The woman had to be a regular, because she and the bartender seemed to know each other. Toni couldn't help eavesdropping as the other woman flirted outrageously.

Finally, the bartender approached Toni. "What can I get for you?"

"Um, I don't—" Toni looked up into the most striking face she'd ever seen, and her mouth went dry. He had brown curls with just a hint of red, and his skin was the same beautiful golden color as the beer the woman next to her was drinking. But his most arresting features were his incredible blue eyes.

"Ginger ale, please," she said just to reactivate the stalled gears in her brain.

A neat row of straight white teeth flashed between his lips. "Come on, I know you can do better than that. What's your pleasure? Virgin cocktails? Something cool with a kick? Or do you want to go for the ten-count knockout?" He laid a drink menu before her. "We have it all at Blue Paradise."

Toni relaxed a little as she studied the complicated drink list. There were too many choices, including a separate category for Blue Paradise specials that were colored blue. She closed the menu. "Why don't you recommend a drink for me? Uh ... something cool with a kick."

He leaned toward her. "Let's see. How about a Blue Lagoon? Very frosty and fruity."

Toni nodded, trying not to appear hypnotized by his incredible eyes. "Okay, but if I don't like it I'm going to hold you responsible."

He winked. "Uh-oh. Luckily I'm good under pres-

sure. If you're not fully satisfied let me know, and I'll
see what I can do."

Toni felt as if her body were on fire. His words were
innocent, but her hormones had their own interpreta-
tion. She watched as he prepared her drink. He wore
a dark T-shirt with the Blue Paradise logo on the left
side of his chest. She couldn't help noticing how well it
cupped his large biceps and stretched across his pectoral
muscles. What a body!

She straightened on the stool, trying to pull herself
together. Suddenly she was very conscious of her own
clothing. The short, black wraparound skirt patterned
in browns and golds was a style she'd normally wear,
but the black camisole top was a bit more daring. It
had spaghetti straps and a dip between her breasts that
would have been risqué if it weren't for the lace insert
that covered her cleavage.

She looked fine last time she'd checked, but suddenly
she was wondering how she appeared to the handsome
bartender. He placed a frosty glass in front of her. It
was filled with pale blue crushed ice, and was finished
off with fruit wedges and an electric blue straw. "Ooh,
it's definitely pretty."

"Taste it and see if you like it. Your sister seemed to
enjoy it."

The straw never reached her lips. "You talked to my
sister?"

He nodded. "Yes. Just a few minutes ago."

Toni placed the drink back on the bar, shaking her
head.

"What's wrong? Don't you like the drink?"

She stared at the frosty mixture, wondering if she
should say anything. Slowly she raised her eyes to his.

"The drink is fine, but I was wondering if . . . did my
sister say anything *strange* about me?"

He grinned. "What do you mean?"

"For instance, did she tell you that I'm a professional mud wrestler, or that I'm in training for the Topless Rollerblading Olympics?"

His gorgeous eyes lit with amusement. "No, she didn't, but it seems you're a woman of many talents."

"Oh no." Toni's face heated. "I didn't mean that I actually *do* any of those things. It's just that she might have . . . I mean, she has this way of—"

"It's okay." He held up a hand to stop her frantic flow of words. "I understand what you mean. Your sister's been telling tales, has she?"

"Something like that." Toni nodded grimly. "She didn't say anything unusual to you?"

"Nope. We had a very brief exchange."

Toni sighed with relief.

"But she did mention that you're one of only eight people in the country who knows the rare and exotic art of Chinese oil massage."

Her head snapped up. "I'm going to kill her!"

He snapped his fingers, looking disappointed. "Darn! You mean it isn't true?"

Lowering her forehead into her palm, Toni moaned. "Sorry, my sister must have missed a dose of her medication. They warned me at Shady Oaks that she may not be ready for mainstream society yet." She sighed. "If only I had listened."

The bartender's rich laughter filled her ears. "Seriously. What was all that about?" he asked.

"April is under the impression that since we've moved to a new city I should break out of my shell and become a wild party girl. Apparently, I wasn't mingling to her satisfaction tonight, so she went around telling men these crazy stories so they'd find me interesting and attractive."

He leaned forward. "I'm sure that wasn't necessary." His simple words had an unsettling effect on Toni.

She licked her lips, trying to concentrate on their conversation. "Needless to say, I wasn't too thrilled about it." She looked into his mesmerizing eyes again. "Is that the most ridiculous thing you've ever heard, or what?"

He smiled at her. "Believe me, working in a place like this, you hear it all."

Toni shook her head. "Obviously there's some truth to that cliché about people telling their troubles to the bartender. Look at me."

"And you haven't even touched your drink. Come on, take a sip. Let me know if you like it. I'd hate to disappoint you."

She picked up the drink, looking boldly into his beautiful blue eyes. "I'm sure that won't be a problem." Then she wanted to bite her tongue. Had that been *her* voice?

Toni bent her head and took a long sip from her straw. The drink was sweet and fruity, with just a hint of alcohol. She nodded. "It is good."

He wiped imaginary sweat from his brow. "Whew! I guess my job here is safe."

She giggled. Ugh! What had gotten into her? Yes, he was gorgeous and charming—but that was his job. Two women approached the bar, and she listened as they came on to the bartender shamelessly. He was a stud, and he knew it. Just the kind of guy who would have no interest in her.

And what did it matter? A guy like that was a heartbreaker. The love 'em and leave 'em type. She wasn't in the market for another romantic disaster.

On the other hand, she wasn't in the market for a commitment this time, either. He was exactly the right type for a passionate affair. She studied his back as he reached up to pull a glass down from the rack overhead. Affairs with playboys were short-lived, but she would bet her life they were fun while they lasted.

Then, as though he could read her mind, the bartender turned around and met her gaze. He poured something that looked oddly like blue beer into a glass and passed it to a woman at the end of the bar. After he gave the woman change, he came back to Toni.

"If you ever do decide to learn the exotic art of Chinese oil massage, let me know. It sounds like something I'd like to try."

Her eyebrows rose. Was he flirting with her? Or was that just wishful thinking? "My sister's crazy. But I guess this proves people will say anything in a nightclub."

He nodded. "True. Especially men. Women don't usually use lines. Frankly, they don't need to. All they have to do is let a guy know they're interested. He'll take it from there. But you'd be surprised what a guy will say to get a girl's attention."

Toni sipped at her drink, curiosity getting the best of her. "Like what?"

"Well, I've worked here long enough to be considered a pickup line connoisseur."

"Really?"

"Yep, let me dip into my mental file." He nodded when he came up with one. "First, there's corny."

He rested his elbows on the bar and leaned toward her. His blue-eyed gaze held hers. "Do you have a map?"

Toni shook her head, a bit overwhelmed by the intensity of his gaze.

He batted his lashes. "Because I keep on getting lost in your eyes." She laughed and he straightened up, pointing at her. "Are you lost?"

"No," she answered.

"I was just wondering, because it's unusual to see an angel this far from heaven."

Toni groaned. "Ooh, that was bad."

"Then there's sweet." He leaned forward again. This time his gaze locked on her lips, and she had to fight the urge to squirm on the stool. His expression softened. "I've had a really bad day, and it always makes me feel better to see a pretty girl smile. So, would you smile for me?"

Toni found herself blushing. Maybe coming from any other man these lines would sound silly. But at that point he could have turned her on reading the Gettysburg Address, with that sexy voice of his.

He continued, oblivious to the effect he was having on her. "And of course there's cheesy." He looked her up and down, snapping his fingers for emphasis. "Mmm, mmm, mmm. All those curves, and me with no brakes," he finished with exaggerated attitude and a wink.

Toni laughed, tempted to fan herself. Whew! It was getting hot.

His voice lowered. "And don't forget dirty."

Oh Lord! She didn't know if she could take dirty.

"That outfit looks great." His gaze drifted slowly over her as he lowered his voice. "It would look even better in a crumpled heap on my bedroom floor tomorrow morning."

She sighed inwardly. A passionate affair with a sexy bartender was starting to sound really good to Toni. Did he know that his pickup lines, though said in jest, were working?

"There's also cute. I miss my teddy bear." He gave her a wide-eyed, sad look. "Will *you* sleep with me?"

"Okay, that one's pretty slick." She'd buy whatever

he sold with that brilliant smile and his sexy bedroom eyes. She needed to cool off.

Looking around, she noticed that a third bartender was working behind the bar, and Blue eyes was giving her his full attention. "Am I going to get you in trouble? I didn't mean to monopolize all your time."

His laugh had a wicked edge. "Don't worry," he said, crossing his fingers. "I'm like this with the owner. He lets me do whatever I want."

"Are you related or something?"

He nodded. "Exactly."

That statement triggered a warning in Toni's head. She took note of the fact that the other two bartenders were wearing uniforms, and he wasn't. She looked at him again. His eyes sparkled back at her. Blue eyes. Blue Paradise?

"Wait a minute. You wouldn't happen to own this club, would you?"

He threw back his head and laughed. "You got me." He extended his hand, cradling her fingers in his large palm. "Blue Cooper, owner and operator of Blue Paradise, at your service."

CHAPTER THREE

"Blue Cooper." Toni repeated the words as she shook his hand. "I should have figured this out sooner. I'm Antoinette. Everyone calls me Toni."

Blue moved around to her side of the bar, settling on the stool beside her. "I hope you don't think I was trying to trick you. I often help out wherever I'm needed around here. The regulars are used to it."

Toni smiled, suddenly feeling nervous. "No, I don't think you were trying to fool me. I . . . I guess I'm just not sure what to say now."

"Why don't you finish your drink and hit the dance floor with me?"

She looked at her frothy blue cocktail. "I need to pay you for this."

He shook his head. "That's not necessary."

"No, really. I'd rather . . ."

"Look at it this way. If I had met you on this side of the bar, I might have come up to you and said something like: 'Hey, pretty lady. Let me buy you a drink. All I want in exchange is the honor of sitting here, drinking in your beauty.' "

Toni laughed, beginning to relax again. "Oh, and do you think I'd fall for a corny line like that?"

He shrugged. "I don't know, would you?"

She grinned sheepishly. "Probably."

"Good. Add that to the list. I just made it up."

Toni finished her drink. "Okay, you get points for originality."

"Does that mean you'll dance with me?"

Why not? Wasn't this what she'd wanted?

"Sure." She stood and he led her inside to the crowded dance floor.

A spicy calypso song poured from the speakers, and Blue and Toni immediately fell into rhythm. Though they danced a respectable distance from each other, she couldn't mistake the sensuality pulling at them like a magnetic field. As Blue's hips rocked forward hers swayed back, adjusting to his tempo. They seemed to anticipate each other's movements, keeping the dance alive with their energetic steps.

Someone behind Toni missed a beat and jostled her forward. Blue caught her shoulders gently in his hands, but instead of setting her away from him, the dance became more intimate. He kept a light hold on her arms as he guided her first backward, then forward. Their bodies were inches apart.

Normally, Toni hated dancing close with men she hardly knew. It was usually only a matter of time before their hands began to wander and she found herself squashed against some unknown, sweaty body. But this time the closeness was welcome. Dancing with Blue was a new and pleasurable experience.

Soon the music changed and they danced apart again, but now they were more comfortable with each other. Blue spun around and twirled Toni as they moved to the quick beat of a Latin song.

"Whew, that's enough for me," Toni finally said. "I have to sit down."

He nodded, leading her off the dance floor. They looked around for somewhere to sit, but the nightclub was packed on all levels, including the outer deck where they'd met. Blue leaned down until she could feel his breath on her earlobe. "I know where you can have a seat. Come with me."

Her heart rate picked up as he led her to the back of the club and opened a door marked Employees Only. This was the point where she would normally back out, but she wanted more than anything to be alone with this attractive man.

Blue led her down the hall and up a winding set of stairs, where he let her into a private office. She immediately moved over to the large window that looked down over the dance floor. "You can see everything from up here."

He came up behind her. "Yes. This is where I work."

Feeling nervous, Toni moved away from the window to give herself time to adjust to the situation. His nearness was overwhelming. She sat on the overstuffed couch, taking in the intimacy of his office.

How many other women had he brought up here? She immediately scolded herself. It didn't matter. No doubt she wasn't the first, and she wouldn't be the last. What mattered was that she was there now.

Blue moved to the wet bar behind the sofa. "Can I get you another drink?"

"Just ice water, thanks." If anything happened

between them, she wanted to make sure it was a conscious decision on her part.

He handed her a crystal glass and sat beside her, taking a sip from a small bottle.

"What's that?"

He held up the yellow label for her inspection. "Yoo-hoo. Best drink in the world."

She laughed in surprise. "What? No Blue Lagoons or other Blue Paradise specialties?"

He took a long swig from the bottle, then gave her a look of pure ecstasy. "No way. If I had my choice, Blue Paradise would serve nothing but Yoo-hoo. Fortunately, my advisors convinced me that it would be bad for business."

"No kidding." Toni took a long sip of cool water. "So you don't drink at all?"

"Never touch the stuff."

Her eyebrows rose. "I'm impressed."

"Thank you, but I do have other vices." His gaze was hot as it bore into her, making her shift slightly in her seat. "Drinking just doesn't happen to be one of them."

She didn't have to ask—it was clear one of his vices had to be women. All he had to do was focus those gorgeous eyes in the right direction, and women would fall at his feet—herself included. Still, she felt her lips forming the words. "Oh? Then what *is* one of your vices?"

A sexy smile curved his lips. He leaned back against the cushions, regarding her with those bedroom eyes. "Well, for one, I'm addicted to Saturday morning cartoons."

"What? Are you serious?" Toni straightened. That was the last thing she would have expected him to say. "Why do you consider that a vice?"

"Because I need my weekly fix." He leaned into her, lowering his voice. "Now this is just between you and me . . ."

"Yes?"

"Well, if I want to sleep in, or if I know I'm not going to be home Saturday morning, I tape them."

Toni placed her water on the coffee table and turned to face Blue head on. "Let me get this straight—you tape Saturday morning cartoons?"

"Yep." He relaxed against the back of the couch, smiling confidently.

"You can't get through the day without Bugs and Daffy."

"Oh no, my cartoons are far more advanced than that." He counted them off on his fingers. "You've got the *X-men,* modern versions of *Superman* and *Batman,* and let's not forget our newest, alien-fighting superheroes, the *Men in Black.*"

She laughed. "Oh, *I* see. It's a superhero thing."

"Exactly. And if you ask me, they're too mature for children. They address some pretty sophisticated issues. I have an entire theory on it. I'll have to tell you about it some time."

Toni just looked at him, shaking her head. She was completely captivated by the boyish animation in his eyes. He wasn't turning out to be anything like she expected a playboy to be. A once mysterious phenomenon was suddenly becoming clear to her. She used to wonder how women could be drawn to players. Toni never understood why any woman would settle for being part of a harem.

But now, sitting beside what might be the best-looking man she'd ever seen, she was beginning to see things differently. She wasn't proud of it, but at that moment she wanted Blue more than anything.

"Cartoons are your weakness, huh? I'll have to remember that. Comic books too, I'll bet."

"Okay, you got me. I confess. I'm a collector." He sipped his Yoo-hoo and studied her. "Now it's your turn. What are your vices?"

She took a deep breath. "Okay, let me think." A little devil popped up on her shoulder and whispered in her ear. The angel on her other shoulder tried to stop her, but the words were already coming out of her mouth. "Black panties."

To her amusement, Blue nearly dropped his drink. "What did you say?"

She shook her head. "It's the strangest thing, but I seem to have a weakness for black panties. Especially the lacy ones. I have bras in every color, but for some reason the panties have to be black."

Toni bit her lip. She couldn't believe she was sitting there talking about her underwear, yet she loved watching the effect it was having on him.

Blue expelled his breath in a long rush. He just nodded as though struck dumb.

Toni held back the urge to giggle. Having this kind of power over a man was incredible. In the past, she'd always played it safe with guys making sure not to say, do, or wear anything that would give them the wrong idea. With Blue, the wrong idea was exactly right.

"I guess everyone has strange little quirks. Now that I really think about it, I don't think I own anything but black panties. Not even plain white cotton."

His gaze went hot. Blue's eyes traveled over her clothing as though he had X-ray vision. Toni uncrossed her legs, and Blue watched her intently. If she were to shift ever so slightly, her wraparound skirt would separate and he'd be able to see . . .

Her little angel took over and she re-crossed her legs.

Blue shifted positions, leaning forward, and she knew what he was hiding.

He cleared his throat. "Uh, have you always been into black, or is this a recent development?"

"That's a good question." Toni felt her cheeks becoming uncomfortably hot. Now that she had his attention, she wasn't quite sure what to do with it. She decided to change the subject before she got in over her head. "This is probably a bit over the top for a first meeting, isn't it? Between my fascination with black underwear and my sister's outlandish stories, you must think we're quite a pair."

He held up a finger. "Ahh, but this isn't the first time I've seen you."

"What are you talking about?"

"I saw you in the park today. I was sitting on the other side of the bench when you came out of nowhere on those skates."

Her hands automatically flew to her face. "Oh no. That was you?"

"Yes."

She shook her head. "Then you must have known from the start that my sister was lying."

"That's right. But I was intrigued with you long before that."

She raised her eyes to his. "Why do you say that?"

For the first time that night she saw the charming glint leave his eyes, and seriousness took its place. "I was drawn to your sweetness."

Toni felt her mouth go dry. Knowing that Blue had been attracted to her before she'd even met him intensified their intimate moment. Her teetering resolve went over the edge.

Their gazes connected, and Blue and Toni leaned in to each other. The kiss was inevitable, but she couldn't wait the remaining seconds for their lips to touch. Reaching behind his neck, Toni pulled Blue down to her. She'd always wanted to do that.

Instantly she knew why. A tingling began where their lips met and radiated downward. She became sensitive to every sensation. The slight friction of bristles under her palm where he needed to shave. His skin, hot to her touch. The soft, moist caress of his lips. Each brush took them deeper. *This* was passion, Toni thought, and she only wanted more.

Her usual inhibition melted away as she tightened her arms around him. A sound of pleasure came from deep in Blue's throat. Then, next thing she knew, Toni was straddling his lap. Within seconds their kiss went from PG-13 to an R rating. And in her present state of mind, there wasn't much to keep it from going straight to X.

Her skirt no longer gave her decent coverage. The material separated at the waist, baring her thighs. Blue reached down and cupped them in his large hands. Her blouse might as well have been nonexistent the way her breasts pointed through the flimsy material. The delicate straps danced around her shoulders, threatening to slide completely off.

Even worse, Toni didn't care. She kissed Blue back eagerly, wanting nothing more than to remove the barriers between their bodies. It was that last reckless thought that sent her into a panic. Darn that angel.

Toni slid off Blue's lap, trying not to enjoy it. She immediately straightened her clothes and backed away from him. "It's getting late . . . my sister . . . she's probably looking—"

Blue inhaled a ragged breath and nodded slowly. "I understand." He remained seated for a moment, rubbing his palms over his knees.

Toni turned away to give him time to pull himself together, and to hide her burning cheeks. Usually, she didn't let guys get that far on a first date—and this didn't even involve dinner or a movie.

"Let me take you downstairs." He pressed his hand to the small of her back and gently guided her back to the main room.

They didn't speak on the way down and Toni wasn't sure how to handle this awkward moment. Should she offer her phone number? Did Blue even want it?

"There she is." Toni spotted April on the dance floor doing a slow grind with a guy who looked like Mike Tyson's evil twin. She made a beeline for her sister, not certain if Blue would follow. She grabbed April's wrist and tugged her in the general direction of the door.

"What are you doing?" April sputtered. "Did you see that guy's body?"

"I saw his face. Trust me, I'm doing you a favor."

"Why leave now? It's only—ahh, judging by that glossy look in your eyes and the extra pout to your lips, you met someone."

"Shut up, April," she said, nudging her sister through the crowd. But as they reached the exit Toni took one last look over her shoulder. Blue was nowhere to be seen.

"Damn, she's gone," Blue muttered as he stared out into the parking lot. He'd been pulled away on a minor emergency, and though he'd rushed back to say goodbye Toni had already left.

He couldn't blame her for running off that way, he thought, letting himself back into his office. His eyes immediately strayed to the sofa. Idiot!

Turning away, he slammed his palm into his forehead. He'd practically molested her after one kiss. What was wrong with him? He was supposed to be courting her. How could he expect to establish a relationship with her or build any kind of emotional connection if he let his hormones run wild?

On the other hand, seeing her in the park hadn't prepared him for how sexy she was up close. On the dance floor he'd been captivated by her legs. So long, firm, and well-shaped. They taunted him from under that little skirt. When they danced close, he wanted to lift one leg up and wrap it around—

Whoa! Blue expelled his breath harshly. Not a wise train of thought. Instead he needed to concentrate on how he was going to make this up to her. After the way he'd rushed things, no doubt she'd avoid Blue Paradise for a while.

There *had* been moments when he could swear she'd been trying to tempt him. Why did she have to tell him she had a weakness for black panties? After that it had been all over for Blue. All he could think about were the mysteries that lay beneath her clothing.

His mind wandered for a moment, and Blue had to force his thoughts back on track. Focus. The next time they met he would keep his hands to himself and behave like a gentleman, no matter how difficult that would be. He had to show Toni that he was interested in more than just a one-night stand or a brief affair. It wasn't going to be easy. Especially since he had no clue where she lived.

Fortunately, Blue was very resourceful. He grinned as he plotted his next move. There was nothing like an unexpected visit to sweep a woman off her feet.

* * *

"I can't believe you want to buy one-ply toilet paper. That's so tacky." April and Toni glared at each other from opposite sides of the counter in Coffee.com— their new Internet café/coffee bar. "Even you can't be that cheap."

"Give me a break," Toni said, taking the supply catalog back from her. There were just a few more details to be taken care of before their grand opening Saturday. "You wanted to order the most expensive kind."

"But I'm in charge of decorating. The toilet paper we choose for the bathrooms will affect the overall ambience of the restroom decor." April struggled to keep a straight face.

"That argument is a stretch, even for you. I'm in charge of supplies, and you know good and well that toilet paper is my department. We do not need quilted toilet paper with little, custom-printed coffee cups on it. Especially when you consider their final destination." Toni laughed. "You'd literally be flushing our money down the toilet."

April held up her hands, accepting defeat. "I'm willing to compromise. Can't we at least have two-ply?"

"Two-ply it is."

"Scented?"

"Unscented, but you can choose *one* color. I can just hear you suggesting we order rainbow colors to alternate according to the days of the week."

April's hands found her hips. "That would be ridiculous. Give me some credit, here."

Toni did have to give her sister credit. Though they tended to quibble this way over insignificant issues, when it came to the big decisions they were completely in sync.

She had to admit, too, that April had done a fantastic job decorating the place. She'd saved them a lot of money by shopping for some of the furniture in thrift shops. The loveseats, sofas, and overstuffed chairs were reupholstered in rich greens and purples—to hide the inevitable coffee stains, April said. Though some pieces were modern and others were traditional classics, they all fit well together.

Toward the back of the store, custom-built computer tables in varying sizes were arranged for surfing the net and sipping coffee individually or in groups. In the front, April created several intimate lounge areas by clustering loveseats and cushioned chairs around coffee tables holding laptops.

The main lounge area in the center of the store was Toni's favorite. Two large, stylish couches, a footstool, and colorful, oversized pillows surrounded a wide-screen Web-TV for special events. A few tasteful pieces of urban artwork done by local artists hung on the walls. Overall, the shop was the perfect depiction of youthful culture.

At that very moment sign hangers were placing a lighted signboard that featured a steaming cup of java with an electrical cord plugging into a computer monitor. The steam rising from the cup formed the words COFFEE.COM.

Toni filled out the supply order form and closed the catalog. "That should take care of the rest of our supplies. Now, on to more important things—"

"Yes," April interrupted. "Like who was the mysterious man you were making out with last night?"

"No, like which one of us is going to pick up the promotional flyers from the printers."

"Was it one of the guys I introduced you to?"

"We also have to put stamps on that box of postcards and take them to the post office."

April leaned across the counter. "Which one was it? The lawyer from Miami?"

"I suggest you go pick up the flyers while I get started on these postcards." Toni pulled the box of cards into her lap, swivelling on the stool away from April's prying eyes.

"No? Well, I know it wasn't the bodybuilder. How about the stockbroker? Did you decide to dabble in body paint, after all?"

"When you get back, you can help me finish stamping postcards. Then I can go with you to distribute the flyers."

Toni could be every bit as stubborn as April. She couldn't talk about Blue. Not until she'd sorted out her feelings about what had happened last night.

The memory of kissing Blue had kept her awake half the night. She'd relived it in the shower that morning, on the drive to the shop, and every time she allowed her mind an idle moment. Last night she'd panicked, but the fact was she'd found exactly what she'd been looking for. Passion. She promised herself that the next time she saw Blue Cooper she wouldn't let it go to waste.

She had nothing to lose. Toni wasn't looking for love or a lasting commitment, so Blue didn't have the power to hurt her. She could enjoy an affair with him, and when it was over, she could walk away with her heart intact.

"I'm not giving up, so you might as well tell me."

"We don't have time to talk about this, April. There's too much work to be done."

The door opened behind them, and Toni assumed

the sign hangers were coming in to let them know they were finished.

"Ahh, it was the bartender," April said confidently. "Good choice."

"Look, I—" Toni gasped as two hands caught her shoulders. She tried to turn, but the hands held her in place.

The man took a deep breath next to her ear. "Girl, you're like a fine cup of coffee. Warm, tasty, and a real eye-opener."

The hands dropped away and she turned to look up into a pair of unforgettable eyes. "Blue. How did you find me?"

He winked at her. "I have my ways."

April stuck her head between them. "I knew you were holding out on me."

Blue backed up and grinned at April. "Good to see you again, April."

She straightened and looked back and forth between Toni and Blue. "So you're the one who kissed Toni's socks off last night."

Blue's golden skin flushed. "That would be me."

April punched Toni in the arm. "Go 'head, girl!" She came around to the other side of the coffee bar. "Sorry I can't stay to see some more sparks fly, but I have to get over to the printer's."

She retrieved her shoulder bag and Rollerblades from a chair in the corner. "Don't worry about the flyers, Tone. I've got my skates, so distribution will be a piece of cake."

"Wait a minute. What about these postcards? There are over a thousand that need to be stamped."

April sailed over to the door. "I'm sure Blue will be thrilled to help you." Then she was gone.

Toni turned back to Blue, stunned that he was standing before her so soon after she'd resolved to seduce him. Now that she had him all to herself, could she follow through with the bold thoughts?

CHAPTER FOUR

"I can't believe you're here." Toni couldn't stop staring. He was even better looking in broad daylight, dressed in a white polo shirt and blue jeans. "Tell me how you found me."

Blue hopped up on a stool beside her. "It was easier than I'd expected. When I saw you and your sister in the park, you mentioned Coffee.com. All I had to do was look you up on the web. Your homepage announced the grand opening Saturday, and the address was posted right beneath it. I took the chance that you'd be here setting up."

She couldn't help feeling flattered that he'd bothered seeking her out. "Very clever detective work."

"I wouldn't have had to resort to detective work if you hadn't run off without saying good-bye."

"I didn't mean to. After I found April, I turned around and you were gone."

"Unfortunately, the crowd outside got a little rowdy.

I had to run out there and make sure everything was under control.''

"I'm sorry I missed you."

"Don't worry, you can make it up to me by letting me take you out for a drink."

She pointed to the box of postcards on the counter. "I can't. All of these need stamps and—" This time when the door opened behind them, it *was* the sign hangers. Toni excused herself to make sure everything was as it should be.

When she returned, Blue had taken the box of postcards and made himself at home on the rug in front of the wide-screen TV. He was busy putting stamps on the cards and placing them in a stack.

She took a moment to watch him. Here was her chance. If he weren't interested, he wouldn't have gone to the trouble of finding her. It was time to plunge right in. No more reservations.

Toni knelt on the rug beside him. "Aren't you the busy little bee?"

"You looked as if you could use some help, and I'm a self-starter. It says so on all my job applications."

She took a stack of cards and a sheet of the self-adhesive stamps and began working alongside him. "What? Blue Paradise isn't bringing in enough money? Are you applying for a position at Coffee.com?"

"That depends. What does it pay?"

A few suggestions popped into Toni's mind, but subtlety was more her style. "Um, how about all the cappuccino you can drink?"

"What? No Yoo-hoo?"

"I know Yoo-hoo is your favorite, but please don't tell me it's the only liquid you'll consume."

He shook his head regretfully. "No, I drink other beverages when I must."

Toni stood and walked around the counter to the serving area. "Come over here and look at the menu board. Our baked goods won't be delivered until Friday, but there must be something here I can offer you."

Blue sat at the coffee bar and studied the board overhead. "Hmm, so many choices. Why don't you recommend something for me?"

"Okay. Well, since we know you're a fan of chocolate, how about a mochaccino? I'll put extra chocolate in it for you."

"All right, but if I don't like it I'm holding you responsible."

Toni giggled when she realized he was repeating their conversation from the night before. She didn't have to think hard to remember her next lines. "Uh-oh. Luckily I'm very good under pressure. If you're not fully satisfied, let me know, and I'll see what I can do."

Blue's gaze had locked on her lips as she'd spoken, and she knew exactly what he'd been thinking about. Toni whirled around and started the cappuccino machine, trying to hide that she was obviously flustered. Clearly she couldn't take the pressure of the direct approach. She was just going to have to act naturally, and see what developed between them.

When the mochaccinos were ready, Toni poured them into decorative glasses and topped them with whipped cream and chocolate sprinkles. She placed one in front of Blue and carried hers over to the rug where they'd set up.

Blue got comfortable at the foot of the sofa and took a sip of his drink. "Mmm. Not as good as a Yoo-hoo, of course, but it's not bad."

Toni looked up and laughed. "You have whipped cream on your nose."

Before she realized what he was up to, Blue dipped

his finger into her whipped cream and plopped it on her nose. "So do you. I thought it was a fashion statement."

A giggle burst from her lips as Toni reached up to wipe off her nose with her napkin. "You're a silly one, aren't you? I can see we're not going to get much done today."

Though she hadn't quite worked up to licking it off herself, Toni felt a tiny prickle of disappointment when Blue wiped off his own nose.

He winked at her, letting her know he'd followed her train of thought. "No, no, I promise to behave," he said, though his expression implied just opposite. Lowering his head, he diligently resumed stamping post-cards. Toni did the same. After working quietly for a few moments, Blue paused. "Speaking of behaving, I want to apologize for last night."

She froze. "What?"

"I know I rushed things last night, but I want you to know that I'm interested in getting to know you. I want to take things slow."

Slow! No, no, slow is bad, Toni wanted to scream. Instead she took a deep breath. "Things did get very . . . *heated* last night. But I take equal responsibility for that kiss."

"Thanks for your understanding, but I just wanted to make it clear that I'm interested in more than a hot grope."

She nodded, continuing to stamp cards, unsure how to respond. Just her luck. Her first sexy playboy, and he wanted to take things slowly. On the other hand, last night she'd hopped off his lap and practically run from the room in a panic. Of course he'd think he'd rushed things. He was afraid of scaring her off. All she had to do was let him know that she *wanted* a faster pace.

The question was, how did she do that?

"These are cool postcards." He studied the collage of coffee symbols and computer images that announced the grand opening of Coffee.com. "Did you do the design yourself?"

"Yes. How did you know? I used to be a graphic designer for Capital Computer Consulting, back in Washington, D.C."

"Ahh, that explains the flashy Web site and this trendy decor, but how did you and your sister get into coffee and computers?"

"To put it simply, we won the lottery."

Blue's jaw dropped. "The odds of that are something like eighty thousand to one. How many tickets did you have to buy before you won?"

"I never bought a single ticket," Toni said with pride. "My sister wasn't trying to be chintzy, so she bought me a lottery ticket for my birthday."

"That's amazing. Just one ticket? I heard a person has a better chance of being stung by killer bees than winning the lottery. Congratulations."

"It was a dream come true. I know it sounds crazy, but the hardest part was deciding how to spend the money. It's easy to come up with ideas when you have no hope of winning, but once the money's actually there, you can't just blow it."

"So how did you decide on the business?"

"I'd always loved computers, and I've always wanted to own my own business. April, on the other hand, had a lot of restaurant experience. So we decided to capitalize on a rising trend, which led us to Coffee.com."

"I'm impressed. The two of you will do very well."

Toni laughed. "If we don't kill each other first."

His comical expression told her he was going to leave

that subject alone. "You two seem to be complete opposites."

She thought about that for a moment. Many people had that impression. "Actually, we're not *complete* opposites. We think a lot alike. The difference is that April usually acts on all her impulses. I tend to err on the side of caution."

Blue nodded. "Very wise. It's fun to watch the two of you, though. I know there's no excuse for eavesdropping, but I couldn't help myself once the two of you got started yesterday."

"I know. We've always been the family comedy act. We can bring out the best and the worst in each other. I can hardly believe we're living under the same roof for the first time in ten years—in addition to working together."

"Why don't you get separate apartments?"

"We're trying to cut down on expenses. April and I are sharing a place until Coffee.com gets off the ground."

Blue snickered. "How's it working out so far?"

"Better than expected, but we have hit a few snags. My sister's a bit of a . . . clutter bug."

"Oh yeah?"

"She has an addiction to The Home Shopping Network and late night infomercials. She's collected all sorts of junk over the years, and now she's filled our apartment with it."

"Like Ginsu knives and Weed Whackers?"

"More like The Clapper and a bunch of goofy kitchen appliances. Hot Pocket sandwich presses. Vegetable juicers. Heart-shaped muffin pans. Can you believe she actually gave me a Chia head for Christmas one year? She never uses any of it, but she refuses to get rid of it."

"The two of you are beginning to sound like *The Odd Couple*. You're Felix, and April is Oscar."

Toni laughed. "We're not *that* bad—yet. But enough about me. Between eavesdropping on us in the park and this conversation, you know far more about me than I know about you."

He spread his arms wide. "What do you want to know?"

She thought for a moment. Where should she start? Then a silly idea came to her. "All right, how about this? My sister is always reading me personality tests she finds on the Internet."

"You mean the ones where you analyze my favorite color or animal, and tell me what it says about me?"

"Something like that. Let me see if I can find the one she read to me this morning." Toni got up to grab the sheet of paper April had left on the counter. She sat down in front of Blue. "Okay, imagine you're walking in the woods. Who are you walking with?"

Blue diligently continued stamping postcards, then looked up and smiled at her. "You."

Toni's cheeks heated. She knew exactly what that meant. They were off to a good start. Mentally, she gave herself a pat on the back. "As you're walking, you come across an animal. What kind of animal is it?"

"A big, black grizzly bear."

She raised her gaze from the printout. "And how do you interact with the bear?"

"Let's see . . . you and I are going for a romantic stroll in the woods. We're laughing, talking, holding hands, just enjoying the afternoon . . . when a ferocious bear jumps out and tries to attack us."

He lurched at her, making her jump. Then he settled back, drawing her eyes to his thick biceps with a casual flex. "Naturally, hero that I am, I must protect you. So

I engage in hand-to-paw battle with the beast until it yields to my superior strength. Finally, it runs off, defeated.''

Toni shook her head at his vivid imagery. "My, you *do* like to elaborate, don't you?"

"It's a personality test, right?" he asked, and she nodded. "Then I have to make my case."

"Make your case for what?"

"Having a personality."

She laughed and continued to read. "Okay, you walk deeper in the woods and enter a clearing. Before you is your dream house. Describe its size."

"Actually the house I live in right now is my dream home," Blue said. "I guess it's pretty big. It's ranch-style—one level. All the rooms are spacious, and I have a patio that opens out to the pool area."

"That sounds really nice."

"I like it. I hope I'll be able to convince you to visit some time."

"Maybe." *Just say the word.* "Next question. Is your dream house surrounded by a fence?"

"Nope. No fence."

"All right, you enter the house. You walk to the dining room and see the dining table. Describe what you see on and around the table."

"I see an intimate dinner setting for two waiting for us. My mother's cherished fine china. Candles. Wine. Soft music is playing on the stereo . . ."

She cleared her throat, for herself as much as Blue. "Now you leave by the back door. Laying in the grass is a cup. What material is the cup made of?"

He grinned. "It's solid gold, of course."

She read on. "What do you do with the cup?"

"I dust it off and take it with me. Could be valuable."

"You walk further and you find yourself standing at

the edge of a body of water. What type of body of water is it?"

"I have a pool in my backyard, but if I had my choice, it would be the ocean."

"How will you cross the water?"

"I'd sail across in my brand new yacht," he said with a wink.

"Okay, that's the end. Now for the interpretation. Let me see . . . the person you're walking with is the most important person in your life."

Blue's eyebrows rose. "Sounds like fate to me."

Blushing again, Toni quickly moved on. "The size of the animal represents your perception of the size of your problems. So apparently you have grizzly bear size problems."

Blue grinned. "What can I say? Running a nightclub ain't easy."

Nodding, she continued. "How you interact with the animal represents how you deal with your problems. Hand-to-paw combat?"

He nodded, tugging at his collar and flexing his muscles. "That's right. I face my problems head on."

"Okay, it says the size of your dream house represents your ambition. Sounds like you're pretty ambitious."

Blue smiled. "When it comes to you, I'm very ambitious."

"And the fence," Toni said, trying to be cool in the face of his flattery. "No fence is indicative of an open personality. People are welcome at all times."

"Sounds good to me." His eyes were an open invitation.

"This part is about the dining room table. If your answer did not include food, people, or flowers, then you are generally unhappy."

"What did I have?"

Toni thought back. "Hmm. That's a tough one. Your food and people were sort of implied, but you didn't actually mention them. What do you think that means?" His answer surprised her.

"Let me think. Am I generally unhappy? No, I couldn't say that I am. On the other hand, I couldn't really say that I'm generally happy, either."

Toni watched him, trying to see how he would turn that statement into a joke, but for an instant, his blue eyes didn't sparkle. They were dark, almost brooding.

Not sure how she should react, Toni moved on. "Now we're getting to the interesting part. The durability of the material with which the cup is made of is representative of the perceived durability of your relationship with the person named in question number one. For example, Styrofoam and paper are disposable; paper and glass aren't durable, but metal and plastic are durable."

"I think gold is just about as solid as it gets." His teasing grin had returned. "I guess that means you're going to have dinner with me tonight."

She lowered the paper to meet his eyes. "I wish I could, but April and I agreed that we would stay in and unpack the rest of our boxes once and for all. Our apartment looks a mess, and we've been doing a lot of running around these past few weeks. We made a pact that no matter what came up, tonight we'd finish it. How about tomorrow?"

"Will you be here again tomorrow?"

She nodded.

"Great. Then why don't I come by around noon and take you out for lunch?"

"I'd like that." She was drowning in those eyes again, so she directed her attention back to the quiz. "Now, what you do with the cup is representative of your attitude toward the person in question number one."

"I picked it up and carried it with me." His look was direct, making her stomach flip-flop. "I believe I was right when I said it could be very valuable."

Toni cleared her throat. "Next, the size of your body of water is representative of the size of your sexual desire."

His grin became cocky. "An ocean. I'm a stud."

"Not so fast, big boy. How wet you get in crossing the water is indicative of the relative importance of your sex life. You crossed it in your yacht. That means you didn't get wet at all."

Blue laughed. "Okay, you got me."

Just her luck. A guy with a sex drive the size of an ocean, and it was relatively unimportant to him. No doubt, if given enough time, she could change that.

He took the paper from her and set it aside. "Okay, now that you're through analyzing my personality, did I pass?"

She grinned. He was just close enough to lean forward and kiss her. "With flying colors."

His eyes darkened and took on a bedroom slant. She'd seen that look before.

She leaned forward. He leaned forward.

Her lips parted slightly in anticipation. His lips parted, too.

"Good," he whispered. "Then get back to work!" He straightened, handing her a stack of postcards. "While you were reading that quiz, I've been doing all the stamping."

Toni blinked in surprise as he thrust a sheet of stamps into her hands. "Right . . . right . . . I'm sorry."

They spent the next hour working amicably and chatting about nothing in particular. She found that Blue had a very easy presence. Around most incredibly good-looking men, Toni usually felt tense and self-conscious.

She also had some irrational need to prove she wasn't bowled over by their looks like other women. With Blue, none of that mattered. It was a pleasure just to be around him.

"Done!" Blue shouted, placing a stamp on the last postcard.

Raising her hands over her head for a long stretch, Toni surveyed the neat rows of postcards they'd stacked. "Thanks for your help, Blue. It would have taken me the rest of the day to stamp all these cards by myself. You certainly didn't have to spend this beautiful afternoon cooped up with me doing such tedious work, but I'm grateful."

"It was my pleasure." He leaned against the sofa. "It would have been another thing if you were hard to look at—warts, buckteeth. Or if you were boring—reciting anecdotes from your childhood. But, fortunately, I'm finding that I enjoy spending time with you."

"Thank you." Toni began gathering up scraps of trash they'd left on the rug. "But since you've done my business a service today, maybe there's something I can do for your business. Does Blue Paradise have a Web site?"

"No. I considered it at one point, but I never got around to looking into it."

After disposing of the trash, she settled back down beside him. "Well, if you decide you're interested I can do the design for you—free of charge."

"Really? I don't know everything that's involved, but I know web page design is worth a lot more than stamping postcards."

"I'd love to do it, and it would give me a chance to practice. I had a lot of fun designing the page for Coffeedotcom. You said you checked it out?"

"I didn't get past the front page. I got the address, and I was on my way."

Toni picked up the remote for the Web TV and turned it on. "Let me show you the kinds of things I can set up for you." She placed the wireless keyboard on her lap and Blue scooted over to sit at her side.

"The first screen is basically a front door. When you go inside you see that we have chat rooms where people can talk to other people at the coffee bar or to people online. We're going to have a lot of special events. We also have pages of coffee trivia, interactive games, and links to interesting sites."

Blue watched the screen with interest. "Impressive. How did you learn to do all this?"

"Reading books and studying other sites on the web. It was a challenge. You could do a lot of cool things with a Blue Paradise site. Music clips from your deejay's dance mixes. Real-time camera shots of the dance floor. Downloadable drink lists from the bar . . ."

"Whoa. Did you think of that off the top of your head?"

"Yeah. I've done graphics for advertising and marketing departments for years." She began typing on the keyboard. "Let's see if the domain name Blueparadise-dotcom has been taken." The web site started loading, and then a woman's torso began to appear on the widescreen TV.

"Oh my gosh." The picture continued to reveal itself. It was a frontal shot of a nude woman with the words Welcome to Blue Paradise barely covering her more intimate assets.

The angel on Toni's shoulder demanded that she back out of the site immediately. Unfortunately, her little devil's voice was louder and she clicked to enter the site. "Well, now we know your domain name is taken."

"I don't know. If I start advertising *this* Web address, no doubt Blue Paradise will be packed every night."

"Well, from what I've seen you don't have any problems packing the club." The next page loaded, and x-rated banners advertised the Web's hottest sites. "If you promote this site, you'll certainly get a different kind of crowd."

Several animated images were simulating intimate acts. At that point Toni lost her nerve. She hit the home button and sent the browser rocketing back to Coffee.com's home page. A hot blush was burning up her cheeks.

She set the keyboard aside. That brief glimpse of naughty Internet pictures had made her more aware of Blue's closeness. Toni was ashamed to admit it, but she was just the tiniest bit excited.

"Anyway, the Web page is just something for you to think about. Let me know if you want to go for it." She blinked, realizing the double entendre in her statement.

Blue didn't seem to notice as he reached over and touched her leg. "That's a very generous offer. Thanks," he said with obvious sincerity.

She felt him enter her space, charging the air around her body as he leaned in to give her an innocent kiss on the cheek. His lips sparked against her skin, then he pulled away. In that instant Toni inhaled Blue's cologne, enticing and fresh as a summer night. Her nipples tightened.

This was the closest he'd gotten to her all afternoon, and Toni wasn't about to lose her advantage. Before he could fully back away she closed in, dragging her mouth over his.

His body stilled for a moment, leaving her the aggres-

sor as she ran her fingers over his cheeks. She continued
to press soft kisses against his lips. In a sudden rush of
motion, his arms came around her, hauling her tightly
against him.

Blue's back was braced against the bottom of the sofa,
and Toni was nearly sitting on his lap. It was clear that
they had a low boiling point. Within minutes they were
sprawled on the carpet. Toni nibbled on Blue's earlobe,
while he kissed the sensitive skin at the V of her red
T-shirt.

Their bodies shifted, and stacks of postcards gave way
beneath them. Toni didn't care. This time she wasn't
going to let anything interrupt the course of nature.

Slow down, her little angel whispered, but Toni wasn't
listening. Blue's touch felt too good. Too right. No other
man had ever made her feel this intensity so quickly.
She had to see this journey through.

His mouth returned to hers. One hand played on her
inner thigh, dangerously near the hem of her white
shorts. The other inched slowly under her shirt.

She sighed. Blue's body felt so—

A bell jangled on the front door, followed by April's
harried voice. "Hey Toni, you'll never believe—Toni?
Where are you?"

Toni and Blue sprang apart. She leapt to her feet and
Blue immediately began stacking the scattered post-
cards.

"What are you two doing down there?" April de-
manded.

Blue kept his back to the sisters as Toni tried ex-
plaining that the two of them had been stamping post-
cards—not rolling around on the floor, making out.

"We . . . we are just about ready to take the grand opening mailer to the, uh, post office," Toni stuttered.

Blue placed the cards back in their original box and sat back on his heels. Toni wasn't a convincing actress, but April was barely paying attention to them, anyway. Instead, she fluttered around the shop in search of bottled water. "All right, fine. But wait till I tell you about this guy I met today."

Toni kept shooting him frantic looks, self-consciously smoothing her hair back into her ponytail when April's back was turned. "Okay, but did you distribute all the promotional flyers? Do you need me to help?"

April hopped up on a bar stool, her skate bag at her feet, and guzzled half a bottle of water in one gulp. "It's all taken care of," she said, waving it off. "But listen, the coolest thing happened while I was trying to unload those door hangers—"

"Unload?" Toni interrupted. "April, you can't think of it that way. You have to approach all areas of this business professionally if you want to—"

"Yeah, all right. So, anyway, I was skating through this residential complex . . ."

Blue couldn't concentrate on April's words. He just couldn't stop kicking himself. He'd done it again. He'd let things get out of control.

As soon as Toni had pulled out that quiz, he'd fallen back into his defensive flirting routine. Deflecting personal questions with suggestive comments or jokes was an old habit. The problem was, in this case he'd meant every word.

He had to find a way to slow things down. This was too important.

It didn't happen every day, but there were certain times in his life when he just *knew* something was right.

It was that inexplicable feeling that, on a given day, could make him turn right instead of left.

Blue was known for being in the right place at the right time, too. Not a moment too soon. Not a minute too late. Precisely on time.

Sometimes it was something as simple as winning free groceries for being the one thousandth customer in line. Other times, it was literally the difference between life and death.

Eight years ago that particular feeling, that sense of "knowing", led Blue straight to an empty lot. That was the lot where Blue Paradise now stood.

He'd had that same feeling the day he met Antoinette Rivers. That's why he had to slow things down. He couldn't risk ruining everything with a one-night stand. For some reason they were drawn together like magnets. Keeping his hands off her was an increasing challenge, but he had to.

He wanted to show Toni that this was the real thing—not just passion. He'd learned the hard way that raw sex could cloud a person's vision. It had certainly dulled his instincts where women were concerned. If that weren't the case, he would have seen through Maria's lies a lot sooner. There was nothing he despised more than lies.

"April!" Toni's outburst interrupted his thoughts. "You were supposed to be passing out flyers, not picking up men!"

"But it's more efficient when you can do both." April grinned wickedly, then ducked her head, swinging her feet around the stool. "Besides, I told you, he works at this center for troubled youth. He got the kids to help me distribute the flyers."

Blue took a deep breath. He needed air. Distance was just about the only thing that could help him now.

His gaze drifted over Toni. He still wanted her. Tomorrow when he picked her up for lunch he'd have to maintain better control of the situation. Maybe he shouldn't spend too much time alone with her until they'd gotten to know each other better.

Blue picked up the box of postcards and walked over to Toni and April. "These are all ready to go."

Toni looked up at him. "Well, it looks as if April has plans tonight despite our pact, so maybe we *can*—"

Blue rushed to cut her off. "I thought I'd drop these off at the post office on my way out. That way the two of you can get back to business."

"Okay, but—"

He reached out and squeezed her shoulder. "I'll see you tomorrow for lunch?" She nodded, looking somewhat confused.

Blue quickly turned and left the store. She'd told him he had a sex drive the size of an ocean. If he weren't careful, they'd both drown in it.

CHAPTER FIVE

Saturday morning April watched Toni run around the shop like a chicken with her head cut off. Her sister's mood had become increasingly foul as the week went on. When Toni went into the back room in search of swizzle sticks, April followed her.

She leaned in the doorway as Toni tore open first one box and then another. "Calm down, girl. I don't think they'll close us down if the customers have to stir their lattes with little brown straws instead of your fancy green stirrers."

"Ouch! Shoot!" Toni ripped open a carton a bit too vigorously and broke a nail. "That's not the point. We special ordered them for the grand opening today. We only have enough to last this first week—we have to use them now."

April snickered. Toni was really in a mood. April couldn't resist the urge to tease her. "Well, I don't know why we couldn't have applied that same principle to the customized toilet paper. I think the customers would have loved those miniature coffee cups."

Toni stopped rummaging just long enough to glare at her. April frowned. She'd thought dating Blue would chill Toni out considerably. They'd gone out nearly every day since they'd met, but April thought Toni came home from each date grumpier than ever.

She made another attempt to distract her. "Maybe I should get my belly button pierced. What do you think?"

Turning her back on the boxes, Toni rolled her eyes at April. "You've got to be kidding."

"No," April teased. "I was admiring Caroline's. She said it didn't hurt, and I hear guys think it's sexy."

"Don't get me started on Caroline." Toni marched over, dragged April inside the room, and shut the door so the staff wouldn't hear them talking. "That girl trained here for a week, and she looked completely normal. Then of course, on opening day she comes in sporting enough holes to make a sieve jealous."

"When did you become so uptight? Other than her ears, she only has three piercings. One in her nose, one in her eyebrow, and the one in her bellybutton."

"I'm not uptight. I don't care if she spends her days off working part-time as a pincushion in a sewing factory. I just want her to look professional while she's representing Coffee.com."

April made herself comfortable on a large box against the wall. "Girl, why are you so wound up? You don't have to worry about the opening today. Everything is in place. We're going to be a hit."

Toni sat across from her. "I know. I'm not worried."

"You're not? Then what's your problem?"

Toni shrugged, absently peeking into the carton beside her. "The swizzle sticks!" She grabbed them and started for the door, but April caught her arm.

"Hold on. You're not going anywhere until you tell me what's wrong. It's not the pressure of this business. You thrive on stress. You should be in nirvana right now. What's going on?"

Toni slumped back down on a crate. "I don't know . . . maybe you're the right person to discuss this with."

"Ooh, an opportunity to give my expert-on-everything big sister advice. I'm all ears."

Toni fiddled with the band on her watch, refusing to meet her sister's eyes. "How do you let a guy know you're *interested*?"

"Is this about Blue?"

Toni nodded.

"Well, I'm sure he knows you're interested. You two have been out every night this week."

Toni looked embarrassed. "That's not exactly the kind of interested I mean. How do you let a guy know you—" She ran a hand over her mouth, muffling the last two words. *"Unt em?"*

April leaned forward. "What?"

"Want him. How do you let a guy know you want him?"

"Ahh, now I see." April swung her legs, enjoying the role reversal. "Hmm, let me think. It's simple really. You flirt with him. Turn the conversation toward sensual topics. Touch him a lot. A brush of the hands here. A rub of the shoulders there. Invite him in for coffee, then give him a juicy kiss he can't walk away from . . ."

Toni sighed, shaking her head. "I've tried all that. It doesn't matter how thoroughly I kiss him goodnight. Or how many times I invite him inside. The touching and flirting aren't enough. He always pulls away and goes home, leaving me wanting . . . more."

"Well it's simple, then."

"What?"

"He's gay."

Toni shook her head confidently. "Blue Cooper is not gay."

"What other explanation is there? You're an intelligent, attractive, sexy woman. What's he waiting for?"

"That's what I want to know," she said, throwing up her hands.

"Why are you in such a hurry, anyway? Whenever I see him, the guy seems really into you. If he's not giving you the big rush to get you into bed, so what? Sounds like he could be serious about you."

Toni stood up and began restoring order to the storage room. "I don't want serious. I want passion."

"Are you kidding me? Since when?"

"Since now. I've wasted a lot of time looking for Mr. Right. I'm tired of it. I don't need a man in my life to be happy. I have goals to pursue, and dreams to live out. I don't need a man for that."

"Wait, I don't get it. If you're not interested in a relationship, what are you doing with Blue in the first place?"

Toni turned to face her. "It has occurred to me that I've never had a romantic fling. You know, no strings attached. Just two people enjoying each other's company, and when it's over—it's over."

April felt as if she'd walked into The Twilight Zone. Toni had spent their adult lives encouraging April to have a relationship that lasted longer than a couple of weeks. "Are you sure you could be happy with that?"

"I'm sure that's what I want right now. Not forever. I just need a change of pace—a break from broken hearts and broken promises."

"I see," April said, though she really didn't. This really *was* turning into a role reversal. She never thought she'd hear herself preaching the value of commitment. "So Blue isn't exactly cooperating with your plan?"

"No," Toni said, tapping a swizzle stick in her palm. "But he will. I just have to figure out how to approach him."

"What if he isn't interested in just a brief affair? From the way things are going, it seems to me he's courting you. Old-fashioned style. What if he wants you to be *the one?*"

"I don't think so. He's a player. You've seen him in action at the club. Women swarm all over him. The only reason he's backing off is that I panicked our first night together. We had a kiss that kind of . . . blew up, out of control, and I couldn't get away fast enough. I'm sure he's only holding back because he thinks that's what I want."

"So you want to show him that you've changed your mind?"

She nodded.

"Seduction. You've got to hit him with the big guns. You've been too subtle. It's time to grab him by the shirt and rip off his clothes."

Toni's eyes went wide. "You really think so?"

April paused. Was this really her rational, think-things-through, older sister she was talking to? "Are you sure you can handle this? You've read more of those self-help books than I have, but I'm sure I've read that sex just isn't a casual thing for most women. We bond with a man under such intimate circumstances. If you aren't in love with him when you sleep with him, you probably will be afterward."

"That may be true in most cases, April, but my heart is in no shape to fall in love. Jordan Banks saw to that. I know exactly what I'm getting into, and trust me, I *can* handle it."

"Well, if you're sure . . ."

"I am," Toni said firmly.

"Okay, then tonight is the perfect opportunity for you to unleash your feminine wiles on Blue. He went to a lot of trouble to invite us to a late night champagne toast at his place after closing. Marcus and I will gulp down our champagne and make our excuses. The rest of the night is yours."

Toni took a moment to mull that over. "That's not a bad idea." She walked over to the door and pulled it open. "Can you hold down the fort while I run out for a minute? There are a few adjustments I need to make to my wardrobe."

"Don't do anything I wouldn't do."

"Why didn't you just say anything goes?"

April laughed as Toni left the shop. She knew her sister too well to believe that Toni could take this relationship as casually as she planned. But, either way, she figured Toni was in for one heck of a ride.

Blue satin, Toni thought proudly as she prepared a tall, frothing cup of mocha mint coffee for a customer. She'd passed a lingerie shop on the way home and had decided that the sexy undergarment was perfect for what she had planned for the night.

Blue satin panties to seduce her Blue knight in shining armor. Her matching demi-bra lifted and separated, creating just enough cleavage at the V of her ruffled white blouse. Her long formal black skirt had a racy split that ended just below the top of her stockings. Black silk stockings with electric blue threads weaving erotically through the lace-trimmed tops. *Blue Cooper, you don't stand a chance.*

April rushed up to the counter and leaned across to whisper in her ear. "We are a success."

Toni moved around to April's side of the counter. "I know, just look around. The place has been packed all day."

"Everything is working out exactly the way we planned."

"Yes, but we may have to rethink our dress code." They hadn't wanted to be too rigid, forcing their employees into uniforms that went against their personal style. So they allowed the employees to choose their own white tops and black bottoms, relying on the colorful green or purple aprons to unify the wardrobe.

"What's wrong with our dress code?" April looked down at her white leotard top and her skirt composed of three tiers of sheer black material.

"I think it was a good idea, but I wasn't counting on the staff having such ... diverse tastes." Their other waitress, Stephanie, had chosen to wear a skintight shirt that left her midriff bare, and her leggings had a line of star and moon-shaped cutouts running from hip to ankle.

"Fine. We'll have a staff meeting or something," April suggested with a shrug. "The important thing is that business is booming. The male customers seem to like Stephanie's outfit."

"Somehow that doesn't surprise me." Toni scanned the crowd. The majority of their customers fit the youthful, stylish, South Beach image she'd been expecting, but a few were a bit rough around the edges.

She looked at the tattooed kids clustered in a corner in the back. "Exactly where did you and those kids from the youth center pass out those flyers?"

April became fascinated with the hem of her apron. "Uh . . . near the center."

"And where is the center?"

April ran her hand across her mouth as she pronounced the name of the street.

"What?"

She repeated it.

"April, that's not anywhere near the trendy upscale neighborhoods I sent you to. No wonder we have so many thug types in here."

"Don't sweat it." April waved it off, tugging Toni to one side as a spiky-haired biker came up to the counter for his second cappuccino. "Everyone's having a good time. That's all that matters. Besides, this proves that Coffee.com appeals to a variety of people. We should be proud of the diversity in here tonight."

"That's true." Toni smiled warmly, noting that nearly every computer was occupied.

"In fact, I even saw a guy who looked just like Jordan."

Toni's heart went cold. "What did you say?"

"Relax, it couldn't have been him. He's still in jail."

"Where?" Toni scanned the crowd again, this time more anxiously. "Where did you see him?"

April squeezed her shoulders, trying to calm her down. "He just *looks* like him, Toni. It's not Jordan. See that guy flipping through Internet yellow pages by the front door? He has on a green shirt. Wait till he looks up . . . there, you see? It's just a resemblance. I shouldn't have brought it up. I didn't mean to get you excited."

Toni stared at the man carefully. There *was* a strong resemblance, but to her relief it wasn't Jordan. They were about the same build and shared a few features, but the man she was looking at had to be at least ten years younger than Jordan.

She expelled a laugh of relief. "Shame on you, April. If I didn't know better, I'd say you believed we all look alike."

* * *

Maybe he was tempting fate with his romantic preparations, Blue thought, walking outside to light the candles on the patio table. Champagne on ice. Floating candles in the pool. Kenny G playing on the stereo.

Luckily, he wouldn't be alone with Toni. April and her date could chaperone his frenzied libido. He knew without looking at his watch that it was nearly time for his guests to arrive.

Blue was looking forward to taking the chill off this big empty house. The deep restlessness that kept him running off on a new adventure every few months had settled a bit in the past week. When he let his guard down, he still had to face the dark images of his past, but being with Toni had made those times less frequent.

Toni. For the past five days he'd been on his best behavior, a perfect gentleman. It hadn't been easy, but the results were well worth it. He and Toni went to the zoo, picnicked on the beach, and slow danced at Blue Paradise. Saying goodnight was always difficult, but they'd established a comfortable pace. They were making a connection that went beyond physical attraction.

The sound of the doorbell kept his thoughts from straying any further. Blue opened the door, and Toni practically leapt into his arms. "We did it!"

"Congratulations." He hugged her tight as April and her date, Marcus, slipped past them.

"My gosh, Blue. This is one heck of a bachelor pad," April said, tugging Marcus through the sitting room to the living room/dining room area.

Blue stepped away from Toni and began guiding everyone outside to the patio. "After we have our champagne toast and some dessert, I'll give you all a tour."

Toni gripped his arm. "Blue, this is beautiful. You didn't have to go to all this trouble."

He laughed, slipping an arm around her shoulders. "Of course not. That's what makes me such an incredibly wonderful guy."

She punched him in the arm and they all sat at the table. Blue served everyone a slice of chocolate Chambord cake with a raspberry glaze and filled four glasses with champagne. He remained standing, instructing everyone to raise their glasses for a toast.

"To Antoinette and April Rivers, two beautiful entrepreneurs, and to the successful debut of Coffee.com."

"Cheers!" They all clinked glasses and sipped the champagne.

Blue saw April nudge Toni and whisper, "Mmm, this is the good stuff, honey. You'd better keep him." A second later, April grimaced, and he assumed that Toni had kicked her under the table.

Toni took a bite of her cake and moaned with delight. "This is delicious, Blue."

"Thank you. It's a little known secret."

Marcus raised an eyebrow. "I do a bit of cooking myself. I'd love to have your recipe. Could I offer you a trade? The Taylor family has a recipe for white chili that will raise the roof. It's been an exclusive Taylor tradition for years, but I might be persuaded to—"

"No." Blue held up his hand. "I can't have you giving away any family traditions. We're all friends here, so I guess it's safe to share the secret."

Marcus grinned. "Thanks, man. I'd appreciate it."

He leaned forward, lowering his voice. "Okay, this recipe involves a lot more than just mixing up a bunch of ingredients in a bowl and baking them in an oven. It requires a real love and appreciation of food."

Everyone at the table nodded, hanging on every word. Marcus had taken out a pen and was poised to take notes on his napkin.

"The most important part of the recipe can only be found in a little shop between Sycamore Valley and Gardenia Avenue. It's right beside a bridge, hidden between two buildings, so it's easy to miss. Go inside and talk to a woman named Edwina. You have to make conversation for no less than two minutes, and if you compliment the smell of her blueberry muffins with a pure heart and complete sincerity ... maybe, just maybe, she'll tell you about the chocolate Chambord cake."

Marcus and April sputtered with laughter, and Toni rolled her eyes. "I knew it. You bought the cake. Is any of that other stuff true?"

Blue feigned a hurt expression. "Of course it's true. Edwina doesn't share her special cakes with just anyone. She's like the soup Nazi on those old *Seinfeld* reruns. She has to deem you worthy first."

April's fork clattered on her plate. She patted her satisfied tummy. "Since there's no guarantee I could pass Ms. Thing's test, you'd better give Marcus and me an extra piece to go."

"Go? But you two just sat down."

"Sorry to eat and run, Blue," Marcus said, standing up, "but the youth center opens early on Sundays. We take a group of kids to church and then we have activities planned for the rest of the day. I told April if she wanted to join us, she needed to get her beauty sleep. Those kids never run out of energy."

Toni's eyebrows rose. "Whoa, April—you're going to church?"

April glared at her sister. "Don't say it as if I've never been there before. Marcus got someone to fill in for him at the center last night so he could be with us at Coffee.com. I told him that tomorrow I'd come see what his work is all about." Toni nodded silently, clearly puzzled by what had come over her sister.

Blue had never been one for "warm fuzzies", but things were beginning to affect him more deeply lately. He didn't have to be Dr. Ruth to see that April was falling hard for this guy. It was obvious that Marcus was a departure from her usual type.

As he walked the couple to the door and said good-night, he was surprised by how quickly a relationship had formed between them. He couldn't wait for the time when Toni looked at him the way April looked at Marcus.

Blue walked into the living room and found Toni sitting on the couch. "You didn't want to stay outside?"

She rubbed her arms. "It was getting a bit chilly out there. I brought in the champagne so we could have another toast."

He started to move past her. "First let me make sure all the candles are put out—"

She grabbed his arm and tugged him down beside her. "I turned out all the lights. Blew out the candles. I put the cake away. Everything has been done. Relax."

He let her urge him back against the sofa cushions and push a glass of champagne into his hand. She curled against his side, looking down at him. He sighed, feeling that familiar rush that came with her closeness. "Okay, what are we toasting?"

She wet her lips slowly, raising her glass. "To fulfilling dreams and living out fantasies." She touched her glass to his and took a sip.

Blue had barely taken a swallow of champagne before

Toni was lifting the glass from his hand and setting it on the table. Warning bells went off in his head. He could see where this was headed, and if he allowed himself to start kissing Toni he wasn't sure he'd be able to stop.

Instead of kissing him, as he'd expected, Toni nestled against his side and rested her head on his chest. Blue released his breath, feeling both relief and disappointment. He slid his arms around her and held her against him. "This is nice."

"Yes," she answered softly. "It's been a long day, and all I want is to lie here in your arms."

Blue felt his chest swell. This was romance. This was what had been missing from his life for so many years. Sex was just temporary gratification. It didn't feed his soul or fill his heart the way this simple intimacy did.

He heard Toni sigh softly against him and her hand slipped inside his blazer, absently rubbing circles on his chest. Every so often her fingernail flicked over his flat nipple, causing a ripple of sensation.

Closing his eyes, he hugged her to him with his right arm, and his left hand skimmed gently back and forth from her waist to her thigh. He felt the smooth material of her long skirt, letting his thumb trace the V of her side split.

His eyes opened and were drawn to the length of her leg and an edge of blue-threaded, black lace exposed by the split. The sheer, black material of her stockings kissed the curves of her shapely limb right down to the shiny black straps of her heeled sandals.

Blue felt his body hardening despite himself. He shifted, sinking deeper into the cushions, and Toni shifted with him, moving up his chest so she could brush her lips against his neck. He fought back a moan as his hand slid down her hip to cup her buttocks. Toni nibbled her way up his neck, across his stubbled jaw to his restless lips.

They kissed deeply for several minutes, and Blue became aware of Toni's fingers caressing his bare chest. He broke the kiss, realizing that she'd unbuttoned his shirt.

"Sweetheart, I think we're moving a bit fast."

Toni resettled over him, straddling his hips. "Blue, we can go as fast,"—she traced a finger from his breastbone to his navel, making him shudder—"or as *slow* as you like."

He reached up to catch her hand before it could travel lower. "Honey, that's not what I meant. We've only known each other a week, so don't you think we should—"

"I think we should do whatever comes naturally." Her voice was as soft as a whisper. Those large, brown eyes managed to look both angelic and innocent, despite her bold words. Her left hand, which had been resting on his shoulder, slid down his chest, pushing the material of his shirt aside. She tugged the tail from his waistband, dragging the edge over the sensitive skin of his stomach.

Blue groaned, letting his head fall back and his eyes close. Gathering his willpower, he took a deep breath and opened his eyes, prepared to slow things down.

Toni had other plans. She was unbuttoning her blouse, revealing the smooth, electric blue satin of a bra that barely covered her full breasts.

His words died in his throat, and all he could manage was a throaty rasp.

"Do you like it?" She let the white silk of her blouse

hang at her sides as she leaned forward for his inspection. "I bought it today with you in mind. Is blue your favorite color?"

It was, but even if it hadn't been it would have become his favorite now. He swallowed hard, trying to remember the point he'd been about to make.

Toni moved off his lap to stand before him. She let the silk blouse slide off her shoulders and fall into her hands as naturally as leaves falling from a tree. Then she trickled the silk over his face and down his chest. Softly. Like summer rain. He inhaled deeply as his nose caught the feminine scent of her perfume in the breeze she'd created.

Then she discarded the blouse on the arm of the sofa and began to walk away. Blue could only stare after her, feeling hypnotized by her movement. She paused and looked over her shoulder. "Is the bedroom this way?"

Blue scooted to the edge of the sofa. "Yes, Toni, but—"

She turned around and continued forward, dipping her thumbs into the waistband of her skirt. "Good, because I have something else to show you."

He stood, unsure whether he meant to stop her or follow. "Toni, wait—"

She continued forward, mesmerizing him with the graceful sway of her hips. "You know how I told you I only wear black underwear?"

An image of her brown skin cupped in black lace and smooth satin filled his mind. He stumbled after her. "Yes?"

She turned to face him again, releasing the zipper at the back of her skirt and holding it closed with her hands. "Well, I decided to try something new today."

"New?" He moved up to her, and she backed up two steps.

"Yes. As I said, I figured blue was your favorite color, so I decided to give it a try." She took two more steps back down the hall toward his bedroom. Then she paused, letting the waist of her skirt dip just enough to reveal an edge of electric blue satin.

Blue moved forward. "Toni," he whispered. "We can't—"

She continued to back up until she stood in the doorway of his bedroom. Then she dropped the skirt to her feet. "We can't what?"

His mouth was dry and his thoughts evaporated the instant he saw her framed in the doorway, wearing only two blue scraps of satin and lacy stockings.

"We can't . . ." Blue closed the distance between them and dragged her into his arms. "Let this moment go to waste." He bent his head and kissed the swells spilling from her bra. Then he picked her up and carried her into the room.

She wrapped her arms around his neck and began nuzzling his earlobe. "Mmm, that's what I'd hoped you'd say."

Blue laid her on the bed and undressed her, then lay back as she did the same for him. When he held her close, skin to skin, he was once again struck by emotion.

He kissed her lips, neck, stomach, and thighs, loving her with his body and with his mind. That inexplicable sense of rightness that was becoming so familiar with Toni was nearly overpowering.

Their bodies rocked together in perfect synchronicity. He couldn't bury himself inside her and take his fulfillment until he'd sent her over the edge more than once. Her pleasure moved him, her soft sighs heartened him, and her body completed him.

As he hit the height of their union, more filled his mind than just sexual gratification. At that moment he knew with more certainty than ever before that this was it.

True Blue had found true love.

CHAPTER SIX

Toni lay beside Blue's sleeping form with tears welling in her eyes. It wasn't supposed to be this way. This wasn't how she'd planned it.

She shifted to the edge of the bed and saw her blue satin bra lying on the floor. Actually, this was *exactly* how she'd planned it. She just hadn't counted on feeling so miserable afterward.

Inching forward slowly, trying not to wake Blue, Toni rolled out of bed. He shifted under the sheets, signaling that he already missed her presence.

"Where are you going, sweetheart?"

Even though it was dark Toni bent to pick up Blue's shirt from the floor and held it up to cover her nudity. "I'm just going to the bathroom."

"Okay, babe. Don't trip in the dark." To her dismay, he reached over the headboard and the room filled with light.

His chivalry only darkened her mood. Slipping on

the shirt, she closed the bathroom door behind her. She'd hate for him to see her teary eyes. Ugh! She sighed. What was wrong with her?

Making love with Blue had been incredible. All the sizzling hot passion she'd hoped for. But that wasn't all. He'd looked at her as though the sun rose and set in her eyes. He wasn't like other men she'd known—self-gratifying and consumed with the moment. In one night he'd demolished all of her negative impressions about men.

What did she know about love besides what she'd read in books? All her past relationships had ended similarly. This time her heart wasn't supposed to get involved. Blue was complicating everything with all this tenderness and romance. Where were all the men who wanted nothing more than hot, steamy lust?

That's all *she'd* wanted, but thanks to Blue, all her emotions were getting confused.

Toni splashed cold water on her face, trying to pull herself together. She had to get out of there. She needed to go home. After a night's rest, things would begin to make sense again.

She couldn't stay in Blue's bed. Feeling his arms reach for her in the dark would be too much. So would hearing his sleepy murmurings. Or touching his bristled face. And waking up in the morning and recreating the most poignant moment of her life.

Panic rose in her throat. All this was already too much for her to deal with right now. She walked back into Blue's bedroom. The blue digital numbers on his alarm clock glowed two A.M. He'd drifted off again and was stretched across the bed, clutching the pillow to him like a sleeping lover.

Careful not to wake him, she picked up her clothes and headed back to the bathroom. Toni dressed quickly,

hoping she could leave a note and exit with little expla-
nation. Unfortunately, when she left Blue's bathroom
for the second time he was sitting up in bed waiting for
her.

"You're dressed. What's wrong?"

Toni shuffled from foot to foot in the doorway, hold-
ing her shoes to her chest. "Uh, I need to go home."

"Why, sweetheart? I was looking forward to having
you sleep right here beside me."

He made quite a picture, sitting there naked draped
in sheets patterned after a deep blue ocean. She wanted
nothing more than to sink back into that bed and drift
off to paradise in his arms.

Instead she edged toward the door. "Since April's
going to church with Marcus, I have to get up early to
open the shop. I don't want to oversleep."

Blue patted the spot beside him. "Stay here. I won't
let you oversleep. My alarm clock never sleeps on the
job."

Toni took another step to the side. "I don't have any
clothes. Or a toothbrush . . . or anything. I'll be in too
much of a rush in the morning."

In the dim light she couldn't see his features clearly,
but his disappointment was audible. "Okay, I won't
argue, but if you must go you'd better get over here
and kiss me good-bye."

She took a deep breath, set her shoes on the floor,
and approached the bed. Was there any hope of escap-
ing with just a quick peck?

Blue's arms reached up to pull her down on top of
him, and Toni knew she was lost. His lips were warm,
moving with slow, sensual strokes over hers. Each time
she thought of pulling back, the kiss escalated.

She could feel his desire rising under the thin sheet.
Her skin began to prickle with anticipation. His hands

stroked her sleeves and over her back. She gripped his shoulders, meaning to push him back, but found herself enthralled with the velvet softness of his golden skin.

He rolled her under him, reaching for the buttons on her blouse.

She dragged her mouth free. "Blue, it's late—"

"It's never too late, babe. Not for this." His mouth dipped to her throat and made small circles with his tongue.

"No," she said, trying not to moan. "I mean I need to go. We have to—"

"We have to finish what we've started, sweetheart." He pulled off her top and freed her breasts from her bra. "I never leave a job half done."

His lips covered her nipple, and Toni squirmed with pleasure. "Blue, we can't—"

His hand slid inside her skirt and began trailing sensations up her leg. "We can't what?"

"We can't . . ." Blue's mouth continued to nibble and his fingers continued to wiggle, distracting her. "We can't stop."

"That's what I'd hoped you'd say."

It was nearly three A.M. by the time Toni finally got behind the wheel of her car. Having a casual affair was far more involved than she'd envisioned.

As she drove, Toni sank further into her sad mood. Her time with him replayed in her mind. Normally, at times like this she would rely on the sage advice of the favorite pop psychologist of the moment. But she'd carefully weaned herself from "What's Your Romance Quotient?" magazine quizzes and *How to Meet Your Match* self-help books. This time Toni was on her own. She'd just have to wing it.

She was still reflective when she walked through the front door of the condo she shared with April. Without turning on the lights, she headed for her bedroom.

Her foot connected with something solid in her path. She tripped, releasing a loud yelp as she went tumbling forward.

Two sharp claps sounded, and the room filled with light. Toni rose to her knees to find April standing in the doorway. A second later Marcus appeared behind her.

Still stunned, Toni looked down to see that she was sitting in a pile of dirt. She'd tripped over their potted palm tree, which was now lying on its side with soil spilling onto their brand new vanilla carpeting.

Toni slowly got to her feet. "Marcus? April, what is—"

"The place was like this when I came home last night. We've been burglarized. I was afraid to stay here, so I called Marcus. We didn't want you to come home and find me gone with the house like this, so he agreed to stay here tonight." April punctuated her statement with a long yawn.

Toni immediately scanned the room. Two short stacks of boxes against one wall had been tumbled, their contents overflowing onto the floor. Looking into the kitchen, she could see that all the cabinets were open.

"Burglarized! What did they take?" She rushed for the phone. "We have to call the police."

"They've come and gone already."

Toni shook her head, sinking onto the sofa. "They've already been here? Why didn't you call my cell phone?"

Even sleepy-eyed, with pillow imprints on her face and freestanding hair, April managed to pull off her trademark look of mischief. "Come on. I didn't want to . . . *interrupt.*" She raised her brows suggestively.

Toni glared at her sister.

Marcus rubbed his droopy eyes. "That's my cue to leave. Wake me up if you need me," he called, trudging down the hallway.

April skipped across the room and folded herself on the arm of the sofa. "So how was it?"

"I can't even begin to think about that right now. We've been robbed, April. How can you treat it so casually?"

Her sister yawned again. "Relax. It looks worse than it is. As far as I can tell, nothing's missing. The police said they were probably scared off before they could get the loot."

Toni threw her hands up. "Great. All that means is that they'll be coming back later to finish the job."

April played with the lace edging her short pink nightie. "The police are going to patrol the neighborhood. They say the odds are against whoever did this coming back. I was too beat to start cleaning. We can tackle it in the morning."

Lowering her head to her hands, Toni was suddenly bowled over with exhaustion. The past twenty-four hours gave new meaning to the words *emotional roller coaster*.

Anticipating the grand opening of Coffee.com had been like that agonizingly slow climb to the top of a first incline. Then she had gained momentum, rushing to the next peak with her far-too-successful seduction of Blue Cooper. From there her emotions had fallen off the crest, plummeting downward rapidly until she arrived home to find her home ransacked.

Rubbing her tired eyes, Toni looked over at her sister. "I still can't believe you didn't call."

"Look, there was no reason to spoil your evening. There wasn't anything you could do. I handled it." April stood up and began slogging toward her bedroom. She stopped and looked over her shoulder. "But, if you really feel you missed out on something, feel free to stay up and start the cleaning. I, for one, am going to bed."

Toni stared after April, speechless. With a deep sigh, she let her body fall sideways onto the cushions. Her roller coaster car slammed into the gate, jerking to a halt. She closed her eyes. This ride was over.

"So you slept with him after only a week?" Her former co-worker and friend, Mike, gave her a piercing look.

Toni rolled her eyes. She was sitting in the office just off the storage room, which she and April shared. They'd equipped the computer with the latest technology so that Toni could update their Web site and take care of other business.

"Don't leer at me like that," she said, starting to wish they were talking on an old-fashioned telephone instead of using an audio-visual enabled Internet connection. "It's not as cheap as it sounds. We spent nearly every day of that week together."

Mike threw his head back and laughed. For a millisecond, the pink internal cavern of his mouth froze on her computer screen. Toni winced. No doubt equally unflattering frames of her were flashing across his screen, as well.

"Back away from the camera," Toni said into her microphone. "I'm getting some close-ups that only your dentist should see."

After a few false starts, Mike managed to make the camera lens zoom out. Now Toni could see the sly scowl rumpling his Asian features. "Don't try to distract me. I was about to make a point."

"No, you weren't. You were laughing at me." She

slumped in her desk chair, folding her arms across her chest. Toni and Mike had worked for the same computer graphics company for six years. It was nice to know the distance separating them couldn't dim the friendship they'd developed over that time.

"I was laughing because you were getting so defensive. You told me yourself that the whole idea behind that seduction scene was to initiate an affair. Sounds like everything's going according to your plan."

"Not quite. That's why I wanted to talk to you about this. I need a male opinion. Even April's going soft on me. She's got a new boyfriend, and suddenly it's hearts and flowers all the way."

"Ugh, you're breaking my heart." Mike lowered his head onto his arms, momentarily filling her view with silky black hair. "I'd always hoped she'd turn to me when she was finally ready to settle down."

"Give me a break. You've got more women than you know what to do with as it is, which is exactly why I need your advice. It's been over a month since Blue and I . . . got together, and I'm just not sure I'm going about this affair thing properly."

Mike lifted his head. "What's to know? Sounds like you've mastered the basics." A few seconds later the stilted image of his suggestive grin appeared on the screen.

She made a face at him. "I'm not talking about that. I'm serious. This isn't going exactly the way I thought it would."

"Okay," Mike said, finally seeming to take her seriously. "What happened after your first night together?"

Toni thought about her answer carefully. She hated to admit that she might not be cut out for casual affairs. But, considering her erratic emotions over these past few weeks, that seemed the only logical conclusion. Still, she chose not to state the obvious.

"Well, for starters, I came home that night to find that our condo had been broken into."

His eyes went wide. "You're joking!"

"I wish. At first we thought nothing had been taken, but later I noticed that one of the boxes with my books inside was missing. The police suspect the burglars were frightened in the middle of the robbery, and grabbed a box at random so they wouldn't have to leave empty-handed. We haven't had any more trouble, but I'm looking into security systems just in case."

"That's probably smart, but now tell me—"

"The shop is doing well, too. We've had a steady traffic flow since the grand opening, and we're even starting to get regulars. We're talking about staying open later on weekends."

Mike held his hand up like a stop sign in front of the camera. "You're trying to change the subject. Come on, Toni. You said you needed my advice, and I'm giving up my lunch hour for you. Just tell me what happened with you and Red."

"His name is Blue, and you know it. Stop trying to be cute."

He raised his eyebrows at her. "Sorry. I couldn't stop that if I wanted to. It just comes naturally." He leaned into the camera until she got a close up of his right eye. "Now get to the point!"

Toni released a deep sigh. "Actually, my problem is twofold. First, I think Blue is more emotionally involved than I thought he would be."

Mike's handsome features brightened. "Okay, now we're getting somewhere. Go on."

"From what I could tell when I met him, he seemed like your average Don Juan. A player. He was super smooth, saying all the right things, and the women at the club were all over him. I didn't think he was interested in anything serious.''

"So what makes you think he wants something more?''

Toni leaned her elbows on the desk. "It's the way he treats me. He's attentive to my needs. Considerate of my feelings. But the biggest sign is that he always wants to talk about our relationship. I've never known a guy who was so interested in doing that.''

Mike laughed. "Sounds like classic role reversal.''

"Yes, and it's making me question my own feelings.''

"Ahh, so you're starting to develop feelings for him in return.''

"I'm not sure. It's just that we seem to have a lot more going on than just an affair. For instance, he calls me nearly every night.''

"Booty calls?''

"Not at all. We talk for hours about anything and everything. He always picks me up for lunch, or cooks dinner for me. We spend evenings dancing at his club. Sometimes we just go on long drives, or he takes me sightseeing. He even agreed to take Rollerblading lessons with me, and he hates skating.''

Mike tossed his head. "Sounds like love to me.''

"Don't tease. It's not funny. I don't think I'm ready for a commitment, but things are going so well between us I just don't want it to end. I'm afraid the reason it's going so well is that I've struggled not to let my heart get involved. If I start to trust what's happening between us, I think everything will fall apart.''

"Toni, have you told him your feelings? Does he know you aren't looking for forever?''

"No, it just sounds so stupid when I say it out loud. All my life I've waited for a man to treat me the way

Blue does. I don't want to cheapen it by saying that I want less. I'm not sure where to go from here."

"Why don't you give the two of you some space? That will give you time to decide what you want. Don't see him for a few days."

"But, Valentine's Day is the day after tomorrow. I can't ask him for space now. He might think I'm rejecting him."

Mike shook his head, and between the blurring motion of the camera frames, Toni caught his look of utter confusion.

"I know I'm not making any sense. I can't figure it out myself."

"Okay, here's my advice. Stop thinking so much. Just sit back and enjoy it, and let the relationship take its course."

Toni stared at him. "You make it sound so simple."

"It is simple. The problem with you women is that you overanalyze everything."

The natural instinct to defend her gender compelled her to respond, but in this case she had to admit that he had a point—though she had no intention of telling him that.

"Do you think spending Valentine's Day with him will complicate things?"

Mike thought about that for a moment. "Don't let it. You started out controlling this relationship. Why did you stop? If you want Valentine's Day to focus more on the hot and sexy and less of the hearts and candy, take the initiative. Call him up and tell him you've got the entire night planned."

He grinned sinfully, clearly warming up to his own idea. "Go shopping in one of those sexy lingerie, etc., stores, and stock up. Really tramp it up. Guys like it when good girls take the night off and get really naughty."

"Mmm. That idea has some real potential. I just may do that."

Mike looked down at his watch. "Sorry, honey, my lunch hour's up. I've got to go."

"Okay, thanks for the advice, Mike. Give everyone at the office my love."

"Sure thing, and don't forget to let me know how this all turns out."

"You got it. In fact, I think I'm going to contact Blue right now. Bye, Mike."

They both signed off and broke the connection. An idea began to form in Toni's head. Giggling to herself, she dialed Blue's number.

"Okay, babe. See you in a minute. Bye." Blue hung up the phone and went into the guest bedroom, where he kept his computer. Over the past few weeks he'd made some serious upgrades trying to keep up with Toni. It had started with a new modem so he could connect to Coffee.com from home. Then he'd bought more memory, and a bigger hard drive. Now he had a fancy microphone unit and a digital camera.

He sat in front of the computer, happier than he'd been in a long time, but one thing was spoiling it. He'd gotten as close to Toni as she would allow, and every time he tried to get closer she pushed him away. He tried talking to her about it, but she either blew it off or tried to change the subject.

She kept telling him not to worry, that things were fine just as they were. Blue knew better. He knew exactly how she felt, because he'd spent the last several years of his life running from relationships. The signs of panic were clear. He was going to have to find a way to ease whatever fears she was having. What they had was too good to lose.

Blue logged onto the Internet and went to the private chat room she'd directed him to. The computer took a moment to read her information, then her lovely, smiling face appeared on his screen. "Hi, sweetheart."

The image shifted, and he saw Toni clamping her hands over her ears. "Blue, I told you that you don't have to shout. The microphone is very sensitive."

He gave her an apologetic look. "Oops. I keep forgetting. I'm still not completely used to this thing."

Her eyes softened, and Blue recognized that mysterious half smile she was wearing. It meant she was up to something, which could only mean good things for him. "What's going on?"

She reached up to play with one of her curls. Another sure sign. Toni liked to wear her hair pulled back from her face, but lately she'd been wearing it down around her shoulders because he liked it that way. He'd noticed that whenever she was formulating a plan she'd pick up a curl and stroke it. It was a very sensual habit.

"I wanted to make sure you had Valentine's Day open."

"We're having a special evening at the club. I have to spend a certain amount of time there. I was hoping you'd join me."

"Other than making an appearance at the club, you haven't made any special plans, have you?"

His eyebrows rose inquisitively. "No, I haven't. Why?"

"I want you to leave everything up to me. I have a few surprises in store for you."

Blue was intrigued, without a doubt, but he'd noticed that Toni seemed more focused on the physical aspect of their relationship. Ever since their first night together she'd seemed a bit off balance. The bedroom was the only place where she let down her guard.

On the most romantic night of the year, Valentine's Day, Blue wanted just that—romance. He had no idea what Toni was planning, but that wouldn't keep him from making a few plans of his own.

JB gripped the telephone receiver tightly, wishing he could crush it with his bare hands. He forced his voice to sound calm. "What the hell have you two been doing all these weeks? And don't tell me you've been in Disney World."

"Disney World?" Barry laughed nervously. "Of course we weren't in Disney World."

"Yeah," Larry piped up in the background. "That's too far away. The beach is closer."

He took a deep breath, loosening his grip on the phone. The temptation to beat himself unconscious with it was strong. "Look," he said, keeping his voice low. "I did not send you to Florida for a vacation. You're supposed to be looking for my money!"

"We know, JB. It ain't like we were on the beach kickin' it. We were, uh, thinking. Right, Larry?"

"Yeah." Larry took the phone from his brother. "We were strategerizing. It ain't like were out there getting our freak on with the honeys. We didn't even *want* to judge that beach beauty competition. Ouch!"

Barry grabbed the phone back. "What he means is—"

"I don't *care* what he means. The point is, you two shouldn't waste your time thinking. That's my job. When you don't know what to do next, come to me."

"But, JB, you're all the way in D.C. If we went back every time—"

"That's not what I mean, knucklehead. I mean you should call me. You're not leaving Florida until you find my money." He heard mumbling in the background as Barry related the message to Larry. "Listen carefully. I'm going to tell you exactly what to do."

JB laid out the plan as clearly as he could, making sure to repeat each instruction several times. He even made them write it down and read it back to him. He felt like a professor teaching a course in remedial con artistry. "Have you got that? Good. Now call me back when you're done."

After hanging up, JB leaned toward the wall and began slowly banging his forehead against it.

A prison guard came up behind him. "Come on, Banks. It's time to go back to your cell."

CHAPTER SEVEN

Toni walked into Blue's office carrying a shopping bag filled with goodies. Blue was downstairs emceeing the Dating Game event the club was sponsoring for Valentine's Day. That gave her plenty of time to set up for the evening she'd planned.

Moving over to the low, smoked-glass table in front of the sofa, Toni began unpacking her bag. She took out a heart-shaped candy dish and filled it with a bag of naughty conversation hearts she'd found in a novelty shop. Toni picked up a tiny heart, and the inscribed message made her blush. Perfect.

Next she unpacked a peacock feather, scented massage oil, and a book of erotic poetry from her secret collection. She'd also brought a cooler containing a bottle of wine and some sensual foods—grapes, strawberries, a creamy chocolate dip, and a can of whipped cream.

After she'd programmed the CD changer to play all

the sexy hits by The Artist Formerly Known As Prince—
Blue hated to admit it, but she'd discovered The Artist
was his favorite musician—and lit a few candles, the
scene was set.

Now all she had to do was wait patiently for Blue's
arrival. The contest would be over shortly, and he'd
promised to join her immediately afterward.

She'd dressed carefully for the evening in a dramatic,
ankle-length red dress with softly padded shoulders and
a mandarin collar. Her hair was freshly permed and
piled in silky curls atop her head so that Blue could
have the pleasure of pulling out the pins and letting
her hair tumble around her shoulders.

Beneath the fabric-covered buttons of her dress, she
wore a pretty silk teddy in virginal white. Folding herself
into an elegant pose on the sofa, Toni leaned her head
on her arm and waited. She couldn't stop smiling, think-
ing about the fun-filled evening that lay ahead.

Toni must have fallen asleep while she waited for
Blue, because she opened her eyes to find him sitting
in a chair across the room from her. She smiled at him,
still feeling a bit disoriented. "Hi," she said in a drowsy
voice.

"Hey there, sleepyhead."

She stretched an arm over her head and began to sit
up. Her feet were bare and they were burrowed into
something soft and warm. Toni was still too groggy to
think much about that. "How long was I asleep?"

His blue eyes sparkled. "Long enough."

"Mmm," she sighed. She casually glanced to her left
and quickly drew back with a little yelp. Beside her on
the sofa was the hugest black, furry, teddy bear she'd
ever seen. "Oh my goodness."

Blue chuckled softly. "I went back to the woods and had a long talk with that mean old grizzly bear that attacked us on our stroll. He agreed to come here tonight and make it up to you. He's even bearing gifts."

Toni looked back at the bear. Tucked in one arm was a beautiful bouquet of lilies, roses, and freesia. Around his neck the giant bear wore a lovely crystal heart. Matching earrings sparkled in his stuffed ears.

"Oh my goodness," Toni repeated. "This is the bear from your . . . your . . ."

"Personality test," Blue finished for her. "Yes. Look on the table."

In front of her, two striking gold chalices were filled with the wine she'd brought him. She looked up at him. "These represent your gold cups."

He grinned. "Exactly. Now you're catching on."

Toni was moved beyond words. Blue had gone to the trouble to bring gifts that were intimately related to their relationship, and she'd been so busy creating a seduction scene that she hadn't even gotten him a real gift.

"There's one more thing."

Toni almost groaned. She didn't know if her heart could stand one more thing.

He walked over to the table and picked up a delicate, little jewelry box in the shape of a cottage. He opened it, revealing a plush, pink velvet lining. A sweet musical tune began to play. "The song is called, 'If I Gave My Heart to You'. It's to represent the house in your quiz. I'm giving it to you, because I want you to know that you're welcome in my home and in my heart any time."

Toni took the box he offered her, feeling moisture gathering in her eyes. "This is so sweet and thoughtful. I don't know what to say."

He knelt in front of her. "You don't have to say anything."

She shook her head. "No, I do. Blue, I didn't even get you anything."

"What are you talking about? Of course you did. There's the wine and the food, and I especially like these dirty conversation hearts."

He reached into the dish, pulled out a handful of hearts and began reading them off. "Bite me. Lick me. Suck me . . . ahh, yes. I intend to do all those things to you. Especially this one." He placed a little pink heart in her hand with the same message that had made her blush earlier.

She closed her hand around the heart, still feeling her efforts had fallen far short of his meaningful gestures. "It's not the same, Blue. The things you brought were so . . ."

"Toni, this isn't a competition. You went to a lot of trouble to set up a special evening for us tonight. I'm looking forward to putting every single thing you brought to good use."

She saw nothing but sincerity in his eyes, and her body began to liquefy in his arms. He leaned forward and gave her a long, tender kiss, then pulled her to her feet. The song "Insatiable" was playing on the stereo. "This is a good song. Why don't we dance?" he whispered.

They moved away from the table and began an erotic dance, consisting of hands, rubbing bodies, and lingering kisses. Each time they came together, a button was unfastened or a zipper undone.

They danced into the next song, "Diamonds and Pearls." Now Toni wore only her white teddy and heels, while Blue sported a sexy pair of silk boxers he'd bought especially for Toni.

Blue ran his lips over her earlobe. "If you tell anyone you saw me with these big red hearts all over my butt, I'll have to punish you in kind."

Giggling, Toni gave the underwear in question a playful tug. "That sounds intriguing. I may have to tell the tale just to receive my punishment."

Leading her to the sofa, Blue picked up the massage oil and the peacock feather. "If you insist, I may just have to give you a sampling of my torture right now."

Several hours later, Blue held Toni in his arms. He felt her shift against him, so he looked down at her. "Are you comfortable, honey?"

Toni stretched languidly against him. "You bet." She leaned up on her elbow. "I had no idea this sofa pulled out into a bed. You've definitely been holding out on me."

"Having the sofabed has really come in handy."

Toni clapped her hands over her ears. "I don't want to hear about it."

Blue pulled her hands away from her head, causing her to collapse against the pillows. "That's not what I meant. You're the first woman I've ever made love to in this bed."

Her look was of genuine surprise. "Really?"

"Yes. I bought the sofabed for the times Blue Paradise hosted all-night parties or special events. Instead of driving home at crazy hours, I can come up here and rest."

She nodded, snuggling up to him again. "Very clever idea." She sighed. "Without a doubt this is the best Valentine's Day I've ever had."

"Same here." He squeezed her shoulder. Looking down at her, Blue still couldn't get a good read on Toni's emotions. Certainly, she appeared to be content, and he felt more emotionally connected to her at that moment than on most other occasions he'd spent with her. Yet he still wasn't sure how much of herself she was withholding from him.

"Can I ask you a question?"

She absently stroked his chest. "Sure. Go ahead."

"I've gotten the impression that you've had some bad experiences in relationships. Is that why you're holding back on me?"

He felt her body tense slightly. "Of course I've had some bad experiences with men. Who hasn't?"

"I haven't."

"Glad to hear it." She smirked at him. Then she looked back down, continuing to toy with the sparse hairs on his chest. "Sometimes I do feel as if I've met more than my fair share of losers and jerks. Initially they always seem too good to be true. Prince Charming, Superman, and a knight in shining armor all rolled into one."

Blue nodded.

"Then they begin to show their true colors. Of course, by now I'm already involved and, fool that I am, I usually believe I can save them from themselves. I used to read every book I could get my hands on regarding love and relationships. I used to think if I read enough books I'd find the cure."

"The cure for what?"

"You name it. A broken heart. A heartless lover. A loveless relationship. I finally gave up on all that. I've come to the conclusion that love shouldn't be something you constantly have to fix and repair."

"What should it be?"

For a minute, Blue feared he'd pushed the conversation too far. Toni was silent for a long time.

"I don't know ... I just don't know," she finally answered quietly.

Blue took a deep breath, wondering if it had been a mistake to bring up such a heavy topic after they'd had such a wonderful night together. Hoping to change the mood, he tried to steer them to lighter ground.

"What about that book *Men Are From Mars, Women Are From Venus*? I've never read it, but women seem to swear by it."

To his relief, Toni did chuckle. "You know it did make some relevant points. It explained that men are from Mars, but I think it left out some crucial information."

"What's that?"

"How to send them back."

"Hey!" Blue reached under the covers and gave her a playful tickle. "You're not trying to get rid of me, are you?"

She pushed him off her, moving to rest her head on his chest. "No, not you, but there are a few of your kind that I wouldn't mind getting rid of."

"Ooh, that sounds like dangerous ground. I'm not going to go there."

"Smart move."

"How about this, instead—we've both agreed that this is the best Valentine's Day either one of us has had. Tell me about your worst Valentine's Day."

"You mean other than the Valentine's Days I've spent alone, eating mint chocolate chip ice cream and watching horror movies?"

He laughed, leaning down to kiss her on the nose. "Yes, I mean other than those times."

"Let me think." Toni sat up and propped a pillow at her back, pulling her knees up to her chest. "Okay, I can remember my worst Valentine's Day ever."

"Okay, let's hear it."

"It happened when I was in the fourth grade. I had a crush on this kid named Gary Roberts. That year he was giving out valentines with these huge, red lollipops taped to the envelopes. Naturally, as soon as we saw them going around, we all couldn't wait to get ours. Most of the parents made their kids make valentines for everyone in the class. So of course, when I didn't get one I assumed it had been a mistake, right?"

"Right," Blue said, although he was already anticipating the disappointing conclusion.

"Exactly. So I gathered my courage. I was really shy in elementary school. I was very skinny, and I wore these huge, black-framed glasses that I was very self-conscious about. Nevertheless, I marched up to Gary Roberts and I asked him if he'd forgotten to give me a valentine."

To Blue's surprise, he found himself holding his breath. "What did he say?"

Toni shook her head, with a slow sigh. "He said he hadn't forgotten. Gary's parents didn't make him bring valentines for the kids he didn't like. As it turned out, everyone got one from Gary except me and one other girl, who happened to be overweight."

"Aw, honey, I'm sorry." He reached over and gave her a hug.

She grinned. "You don't have to feel too bad. My sister went to school with Gary Robert's little sister. It seems Gary hit his peak in fourth grade. These days he's fat, bald, and makes his living as a roach exterminator."

"Ahh. Well, it serves him right."

"Exactly. Now tell me yours."

"Okay, let's see." As Blue combed through his mental archives, it suddenly hit him that the last time he'd seen Maria had been Valentine's Day. The last thing he wanted to do was dredge up his past with her.

"Blue? What's wrong?" Obviously Toni was picking up on his negative vibes.

He should have thought more carefully before he'd suggested they have this discussion. Blue reached out and pulled her into his arms. "The truth is, Toni, I've had very few Valentine's Days that were special at all. I guess that's why spending this time with you tonight means so much to me."

He looked down to see why she didn't respond right away. She met his gaze with a look of wonder. "Did you take a course?"

"A course? In what?"

"In charm. Somehow you always manage to come up with just the perfect thing to say." Her features took on a comical expression. "Frankly, I say it just ain't natural."

He squeezed her close, chuckling. "What can I say? You inspire me."

"Pssh. There you go again."

He reached across the bed and picked up a book. "And right now, you're inspiring me to read you a little erotic poetry."

Toni tucked herself against his side, and Blue opened the book to a random page and began to read.

"Your lips, your thighs, your hot, breathy sighs. Your breasts, your hips, your velvet nether—"

Toni snatched the book from his hand and threw it over her shoulder. "Forget poetry. I've decided that I prefer *performance* art."

The next evening, Blue dominated Toni's thoughts as she drove home from work. The more time she spent with him the more fabulous he seemed, and the more terrified she felt.

No man could possibly be that wonderful, she thought, turning into her complex. And if by some miracle Blue did happen to be that wonderful, then there had to be a crazy uncle in the attic that no one talked about. Or a cousin doing hard time in the county prison.

It wasn't Toni's nature to be so cynical about love, but she'd learned the hard way. Whenever she gave her heart freely, she was only opening herself up for a disappointment more devastating than her last. So far, Blue was the most fantastic man she'd ever met, which meant if he were to let her down it would be the grand-father of all letdowns.

Toni knew she wasn't up for it. Especially after Jordan. On the other hand, what if she pushed away her only shot at true happiness because of her fears?

Mike and April had both instructed her to stop wor-rying so much and just enjoy it. If only she could. Toni's emotions were so confused that she knew there was little hope for her to make sense of this any time soon. Her best course of action was to take some time off. She needed to think things through without Blue's presence to distract her.

Next time she spoke with Blue, she planned to ask him for some space. Better that than make a decision about her future that she'd later regret. It if wasn't painfully obvious before, it had become obvious last night. What she and Blue shared could not be regarded as a simple affair.

In her heart, she knew exactly what it was. Toni just wasn't ready to face that reality just yet.

When she parked her car in front of her condo, the digital display on her car radio read 10:45 P.M. She knew April would be staying with Marcus that night, so she was looking forward to having the place to herself.

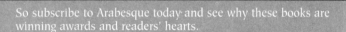

WE HAVE 4 FREE BOOKS FOR YOU!

(If the certificate is missing below, write to: Zebra Home Subscription Service, Inc., 120 Brighton Road, P.O. Box 5214, Clifton, New Jersey 07015-5214)

FREE BOOK CERTIFICATE

Yes! Please send me 4 **Arabesque** Contemporary Romances without cost or obligation, billing me just $1.50 to help cover postage and handling. I understand that each month, I will be able to preview 4 brand-new **Arabesque** Contemporary Romances FREE for 10 days. Then, if I decide to keep them, I will pay the money-saving preferred subscriber's price of just $16.00 for all 4...that's a savings of almost $4 off the publisher's price + $1.50 for shipping and handling. I may return any shipment within 10 days and owe nothing, and I may cancel this subscription at any time. My 4 FREE books will be mine to keep in any case.

Name _____

Address _____ Apt. _____

City _____ State _____ Zip _____

Telephone ( ) _____

Signature _____ AR0299
(If under 18, parent or guardian must sign.)

Terms and prices subject to change. Orders subject to acceptance by Zebra Home Subscription Service, Inc. . Zebra Home Subscription Service, Inc. reserves the right to reject or cancel any subscription.

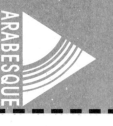
AFFIX
STAMP
HERE

ZEBRA HOME SUBSCRIPTION SERVICE, INC.

120 BRIGHTON ROAD

P.O. BOX 5214

CLIFTON, NEW JERSEY 07015-5214

BUSINESS REPLY MAIL

FIRST-CLASS MAIL   PERMIT NO. 272   RED OAK, IA

POSTAGE WILL BE PAID BY ADDRESSEE

heart&soul

P O BOX 7423
RED OAK IA 51591-2423

She grabbed her purse and her in-line skates from the front seat of her car. Blue hadn't been able to attend their afternoon Rollerblading class that day because of an emergency at the club. It was just as well, Toni thought as she walked up to the cluster of mailboxes. She was still reeling from their intimacy the night before. The more distance they kept, the better she'd be able to think things through.

Toni was so deep in thought that it took her a moment to notice the red Wrangler truck that had just pulled up beside her. In the dim light it was difficult to see the occupants, but she could see two black men sitting in the cab. The one closest to her stared unabashedly.

She didn't recognize the vehicle. No doubt they were visitors of her neighbors. Instead of pulling into one of three empty spaces in the lot, the truck continued to linger. Toni rounded the mailboxes and heard a car door slam behind her.

Trying to remain casual, she glanced over her shoulder. A young man wearing a black, hooded sweatshirt had gotten out of the truck and was heading her way. Remembering the breakin weeks earlier, Toni veered left and headed in the opposite direction from her house.

The hooded figure followed, and the other man edged forward in the truck. Toni quickened her pace, crossing the parking lot and slipping through the path between two condo buildings.

Knowing she'd feel foolish if she'd dashed off in a panic over nothing, Toni stopped and turned. The man continued to pursue her. The truck made a U-turn— she assumed to meet her when she came out of the lot on the other side.

Toni immediately spun around and took off in a run. If she ran into the lot on the opposite side, she'd be trapped between the two men. She didn't know what they wanted, but she was certain the weren't interested in inviting her to the next condo meeting.

The condos formed a simplified maze on that side of the complex, so instead of heading straight across to the parking lot, Toni veered right. Ducking behind a well-groomed hedge, she curled her body into a ball and tried not to move.

She saw a pair of bright white sneakers jog past her. Unfortunately the buildings came to a dead end up ahead, and in less than a minute her assailant would be heading back in her direction. The bushes wouldn't provide sufficient coverage at that angle, especially with a streetlamp spotlighting the immediate area.

Worried about her ability to outrun the man on foot—and his partner in the truck—Toni made a quick decision. Pulling off her shoes, she quickly laced up her skates, tucking the shoes and the bag back in the bushes. She threw her purse over her head and slung the strap across her chest. Stepping shakily across the fresh mulch, Toni hit the pavement and was off.

She heard someone cry out behind her as the man began running after her. Amazed by how far she'd progressed after just a few lessons, Toni skated around the corner and back toward the lot where her car was parked.

By the time she'd reached the curb the pursuer on foot was at her back, and the red truck was pulling up in front of her. There was no way she'd make it to her front door.

Taking a deep breath, Toni jumped off the curb, made a precariously sharp turn, and skated past the truck. Pumping her legs to gain speed, she headed through the maze of lots, hoping to make it out of the complex before they caught up with her.

Toni rounded a sharp turn, barely maintaining her balance, and found herself headed directly toward a pair of headlights. In a panic, she dove for the grass on her right, hitting the ground hard. She heard the squeal of tires and looked up to see the hooded figure careen into the path of the already swerving car.

The car jerked hard to the right, jumping the curb, narrowly missing the man. The pursuer tripped and rolled across the lot, once again into the path of an oncoming car. The second driver slammed on the brakes just two feet from the assailant's head.

Stunned and shaky, Toni pulled herself to her feet. The sound of skidding tires and shattering glass caught her attention. The red truck had rounded the bend at full speed, colliding headlong with the second vehicle. She saw her would-be mugger crawling on his hands and knees to the sidewalk.

An irate businessman who had been driving the vehicle the truck had just smashed into climbed out of the car, instantly turning the air blue. The young woman who had jumped the curb also got out of her car. She'd obviously been out on the town in her micro mini and a gauzy shirt that revealed her bra. She took two shaky steps and burst into tears. All three men rushed to comfort her.

Hoping the commotion would distract her pursuers long enough for them to forget whatever nefarious plans they'd had for her, Toni rolled into the street and began booking toward the main road. She heard someone yell for her to stop, but this time Toni didn't.

At the mouth of the street she removed her skates and jogged across the street to a twenty-four-hour convenience store. Toni didn't know who was after her or why, but she had no intention of staying in one place long enough to find out.

Toni entered the store and headed for the back. She squatted down behind a rack of feminine hygiene products and dug into her purse for her cellular phone. At this rate, she didn't even know when it would be safe to go home again.

Blue answered the phone with his customary greeting. "True Blue, at your service."

"I'm sick of ringing you up and hearing that same tired greeting. True Blue. Why not switch it up a bit? How about saying aqua Blue or baby Blue once in a while?"

Blue immediately recognized the British accent belonging to his best friend in the world. "Jax! You old dog." The man had loosened up considerably since he'd found love. Up until nearly a year ago, hearing his friend boldly teasing and cracking jokes would have been unheard of.

"The one and the only. No doubt I'm interrupting something. What manner of debauchery are you into now?"

"Well, you know me, Friday's a slow night. I have Bambi and the twins preparing my bath and heating the massage oil."

"And seriously?"

Funny you should mention it. I've been seeing someone, and you won't believe this, but I think it's getting serious."

"You must be joking. Don't tell me the great American lover is going out of business."

"Come on, Jax. You know it was never all that." Blue heard laughter in the background, and Jax excused himself and covered the phone for a minute.

"Coco wants me to tell you that if you're thinking of

settling down, you'd better not dream of doing it without her direct approval."

"Oh, she does, does she?"

"Yes, so enough with pleasantries. We're thinking of heading down there for a bit of a visit."

"Fantastic. I'd love you both to meet Toni. She's incredible."

"It's set, then. Expect us tomorrow evening."

Blue laughed into the phone. "You don't waste any time, do you?"

"What would be the point? We aren't interrupting your plans, are we?"

"No way, buddy. You know you and Coco are welcome anytime." His call waiting signal beeped. "Hold on a sec, that's my line."

He clicked over. "True aqua Blue, baby."

There was an extended pause on the other line. Finally, a hesitant voice asked, "Blue?"

"Toni? It's me. I was just being silly. I was talking to an old friend and—"

"I need you to come get me!"

He immediately registered the panic in her voice. "What happened? Where are you?"

"I'm across the street from my condo complex at the Shop-n-Save. Two men were chasing me. I don't know why, but there was an accident—"

"Oh my gosh. Were you hurt?"

"I'm okay—I'm just afraid to go home. I don't know if they're still out there. It was dark . . . and all the cars—"

"Stay right where you are. I'm on my way." Blue hung up the phone and headed for the door, barely registering that he hadn't said good-bye to Jax.

CHAPTER EIGHT

Toni sat huddled on her living room sofa, trying, unsuccessfully, not to dwell on the evening's events. Clicking the remote, she bounced from station to station looking for programming that didn't include a shoot-out, stabbing, or barroom brawl. She'd finally settled on *Nick at Night*, which should have been a safe choice. Unfortunately, this particular rerun of *Happy Days* featured Fonzi staring down angry gang members.

The front door opened and Toni jumped so high that she felt she could have touched the ceiling.

"I found your bag and your shoes," Blue said, closing the door behind him. "I checked out the neighborhood. Everything's quiet now. The accident has been cleared away, but I saw the shattered glass where it happened."

Toni nodded, rubbing her upper arms. She'd changed into a pair of jeans and a sweatshirt, but she just couldn't shake the chill.

Blue sat down beside her, reaching out to pull her close. "Are you all right, sweetheart?"

"I'm doing better now. I just can't stop wondering what those men wanted from me. Could it be related to the breakin a few weeks ago?"

"That's a question for the police. We'll file a report in the morning." He placed a throw pillow in his lap, urging her to lie down.

She curled up her body and rested her head on the pillow. His fingers stroking her hair and caressing her temple soothed her frazzled nerves. She didn't even question his use of the word "we".

Just a few hours earlier, she'd made the decision to take some time off from Blue. Then this had happened. Her first instinct had been to turn to Blue. True Blue. She'd known she could count on him. She'd never been so happy to see anyone in all her life as when he picked her up in that convenience store. Each time the door chimes sounded as someone entered the Shop-n-Save, Toni had gone into a panic. She'd half expected to see the two hooded men who had chased her.

"The police," she said. "Are you sure they're not going to think I'm some hysterical woman who panicked over nothing? I can't prove those two men were after me." She could feel Blue's body tense. His fingers stopped stroking her brow.

"You don't have to be able to prove anything. The evidence is clear. You went one direction, so did they. When you changed directions, they followed. Your neighbors can back you up because of the accident. In fact, they can probably make a positive identification. If we're really lucky, they may have even exchanged information. I'll bet we'll find out exactly who your attackers are by the end of the day tomorrow."

"You're right. I hadn't thought of that. It seems that accident may have saved my life in more ways than one."

Blue was silent for a long time, and Toni could sense that he was worried. "I want you to be careful. Until we get this thing sorted out, I want you to stay close. Since April won't be home tonight, I'm going to sleep here."

Toni didn't protest. She hadn't been looking forward to staying in the house alone.

"Are you working tomorrow?"

"No, it's my day off."

"Good. We can get up and go to the police station together." Blue smacked his forehead. "I forgot about Coco and Jax."

"Cocoa jacks?" She sat up to face him. "What is that? Cereal? I might have some corn flakes."

"No," Blue said, chuckling. "Coco and Jax are my friends. They called just before you did to tell me they're coming into town. I really want you to meet them."

"When are they getting here?"

"Tomorrow night."

"Whoa. They don't waste any time, do they?"

"That's what I said."

Toni found herself giggling. "Coco, Jax, Blue—where did you all get these names?"

"They're nicknames. Jax is the only one who doesn't give out his first name."

"What is it? Something embarrassing?"

"If I told you, he'd have to kill you," Blue said, laughing. "Coco's real name is Cornelia, but trust me, Coco suits her better."

"And you, Mr. Blue," she said, looking at him closely. "It's obvious that they call you Blue because of those gorgeous eyes. What's *your* real first name?"

He grinned. "It's not a secret."

"Okay . . . let's hear it."

Instead of answering her Blue reached into the back pocket of his jeans and pulled out his wallet. He handed her his driver's license.

Toni took it, eager to read the name. "Christopher Michael Cooper." She looked up at him. "I guess I can see you as a Chris."

"Can you? I haven't heard anyone call me Chris since high school. I can't guarantee that I'd answer to the name now."

"That's okay. I'm rather attached to the name Blue." She reached up to stroke his cheek, which was becoming rough with stubble.

Blue picked up the remote and clicked off the TV. "Come on, let's get you to bed. You've had a long day. I'll help you fall asleep with my special True Blue hot oil rub."

She let him lead her by hand to her bedroom. "Mmm, that sounds wonderful."

"Okay, take off your clothes and get into bed. I'm just going to take a quick shower, and I'll be right out."

Toni undressed and nestled under the covers. Now she couldn't help feeling relieved that she hadn't had that little talk with Blue, after all. It was time to face facts. She was in love with Blue.

How could she not be? He was dependable, warm, generous, loving, and unbelievably sexy. He'd given her no reason to believe he was anything like the others.

In retrospect, she could look back on all her failed relationships and see warning signs.

The aerospace engineer she'd dated had seemed a bit on the boring side, but ultimately a good catch. The fact that he made a good living yet never had any money should have been a tip-off to his gambling habits.

And then there was the computer programmer who'd

had enough girlfriends to start his own harem. The fact that he got phone calls at all hours of the night and only received them in the bathroom was a sure sign that he'd been up to no good.

Finally, there had been Jordan Banks, a.k.a. Jason Bonner, a.k.a. James Bittle—known to one and all as JB, con artist extraordinaire. The worst of her romantic calamities. He'd been a fast talker, smoother than glass. Whenever she questioned something that didn't quite add up, he was ready with an answer before she could complete the thought. He'd been on point in every area. Without a doubt he'd been too good to be true.

But she couldn't pass judgement on Blue just because Jordan Banks had turned out to be a genuine criminal with a shady past. Blue was a hardworking man with a good heart. He'd never given her any reason to doubt his past, or his future. She owed it to him to trust him.

True Blue. His name said it all.

"We got some bad news, bruh," Barry said, quietly.

JB rolled his eyes. What other type of news could it be, coming from his two idiotic siblings? "Spit it out."

"We totaled the truck."

"You did what? My brand-new Wrangler?"

"Yeah, that's the one."

"I'll kill you both!" He saw the guard give him a warning look, so he forced himself to take a deep breath. "What I mean . . . is . . . what happened? Was anyone hurt?" JB asked with mild hopefulness.

"Nah, man, don't worry. Me and Larry are fine. Well, Larry got a little banged up when he rolled across the pavement, but other than that—"

"Just tell me what happened," JB said through

clenched teeth. "Did you at least find what I sent you for?"

"Sorry, JB. We tried. We waited for her to come home just like you said to. When she got out of her car Larry tried to approach her, but she ran off. He chased her, but she wouldn't stop."

"I've run that con a hundred times. It nearly always works. How were you dressed?"

"We wore black jeans and black sweatshirts with hoods. Just like they do on TV," Barry said with obvious pride.

JB made a noise of exasperation. "Well, of course she ran off, you morons. I told you to talk to her, not mug her. You were supposed to wait for her to go *inside*, then knock on her door pretending to be her new neighbors. Once you were in, *then* you could find out about my bonds. It was a very simple operation. I thought I told you to write it down."

"We *did* write it down," Barry said indignantly. "We just forgot to read it," he finished in a quiet voice.

If JB had been allowed to have sharp objects, he would have plunged one straight through his heart at that moment. "Just tell me how you wrecked my truck."

Barry launched into a long, convoluted account of the events leading up to a three-car accident.

JB's gut tightened. Instinct told him the story could only get worse. "Please tell me that after the accident you and Larry jumped into the truck and took off before anyone could identify you."

"But, JB, we couldn't leave the scene of an accident. You can go to jail for stuff like that. No offense," Barry added. "We had to exchange information first."

"Of course you did," JB said, defeated. He slumped against the wall. It was hopeless. He might as well resign himself to losing a cut of the money and bring in someone to do the job properly. His brothers were only making things worse.

"You'd be proud of us, though, JB. We knew you wouldn't want them to know who we were, so I thought fast on my feet."

"You gave them the wrong information?"

There was a long pause. "Oh, I guess that would have worked, too."

JB began losing his patience again. "If you didn't give them the wrong information, what the hell did you do?"

"I let Larry write down the information. The way he writes he there's no way those people will be able to make out his handwriting."

JB swore savagely. "If you two one-brain-sharing, double the pressure, double the problems, shouldn't-have-been-born-in-the-first-place twin fools don't carry your asses back to Washington, D.C., right this minute, I'll come down there and get you myself. There's nothing left for you to ruin. Just get out of there."

"What did he say?" Larry asked in the background.

"I think he's mad," Barry answered.

"Ughhhhh!" JB slammed down the phone. If you wanted something done right, you had to do it yourself.

Saturday evening, Toni paused outside Blue's private office to smooth her dress and check her hair. After they left the police station that morning all Blue could talk about were his friends, Jax and Coco. She wanted to make a good impression. Taking a deep breath, she opened the door and walked inside.

The first person Toni saw was a sprightly young woman with bouncy, dark curls, perched on the arm of the sofa. She wore a gauzy, white sundress which was both cool and classic, flattering her dusky skin. As soon as the other woman spotted Toni in the doorway she stood, crossing the room to meet her.

"Toni. I can't tell you how excited I am to meet you." The lovely, petite woman radiated friendship the way the sun radiated heat.

"Thanks," Toni said, instantly relaxing. "I've heard a lot about you, too. Blue has talked about little else since he heard you two were coming."

Coco took Toni's hands in hers and squeezed them. Then she looked over her shoulder. "Blue, I can already tell she's too good for you."

By now, Blue had crossed the room and gently extracted Toni from Coco's grasp. In a stage whisper he said, "Don't listen to anything she says to you. Lies, all lies."

Coco gave her an impish grin and a sly wink, as if to say, "We'll talk later, girl."

Blue guided her toward the sofa. At that point Toni noticed Jax—though she didn't know how she could have missed him. He was standing by the bar, his presence seeming to fill the room. Well above six feet tall, he made everyone else look tiny by comparison. Despite his initially intimidating demeanor, Jax was darkly handsome with his clean-shaven head, neat mustache and goatee. A gold hoop earring gleamed from one earlobe. His expensive, tan suit complemented his dark features.

"Toni, I'd like you to meet my best friend, Jax. Rumor has it I'm this man's only living friend."

"It's a pleasure." Jax extended his hand to her and Toni accepted, gazing warily at his stoic features. For an instant she feared Blue had offended him with his comment.

Then, to her relief, the giant gave Blue a brotherly clap on the back. "That may very well be true, Blue, my man. But I wouldn't press my luck, if I were you.

When I tire of your irksome ways, I may see fit to lower the count to zero."

Toni gasped when she heard his voice. "You're British."

"You're quite right."

Coco stepped into the middle of their cluster and pulled Toni down beside her on the couch. "Now that the introductions have been made, let's get down and dirty. How long have the two of you been together? When and where did you meet? I want to know everything. I never thought I'd see the day that our dear old Blue, the last of the die-hard bachelors, would settle down."

"Really," Toni said, crossing her legs and making herself comfortable. She began to realize that this was an opportunity to get a new perspective on "True Blue". "I'll tell all if you will, Coco. Tell me more about our last die-hard bachelor. I'm all ears."

Blue immediately wedged himself between the two women on the sofa. "Oh no, I'm not letting the two of you get started. There will be no girl talk tonight. Coco isn't happy unless she's stirring up trouble."

"How can you say that?" Coco protested.

"Shoot, I've known you less than a year, and you've gotten into more jams during that time than anyone else I know." He met Jax's eyes with a knowing grin.

Toni listened with fascination. "You've known Coco for less than a year? The way you talk about them, I thought you'd known her for years."

"Jax and I go way back. The reason it seems like I've known Coco for years is because we had a lot of concentrated time to get to know each other this past summer."

Toni's eyebrows rose. "Is that so?"

Coco shook her head, making her curls bounce. "Last

summer was an adventure, to say the least. My brother was framed for a shooting that my ex-boyfriend, Adrian, was actually responsible for.''

Toni gasped in surprise.

"I didn't know it at the time, but I suspected Adrian knew more than he was saying, so I took it upon myself to follow his photography book tour from state to state, trying to get the truth out of him."

"Whoa. How did you manage that?"

Coco narrowed her eyes at Jax. "It wasn't easy, thanks to these two. They were Adrian's 'bodyguards', so to speak."

Toni gave Blue a puzzled look. "You worked as a bodyguard?"

He shrugged. "Unofficially. I was just doing a favor for Jax, who in turn was doing a favor for Adrian's father."

Coco quirked her lips. "Well, for a couple of guys doing pro bono work, they certainly took their jobs seriously."

"So how were you able to help your brother if Jax and Blue were working for the other team?" Toni asked.

"They didn't know the circumstances up front. As time went on, it became more clear that Adrian and his father were involved. Jax and Blue switched teams and decided to help me out."

"We didn't have a choice," Blue jumped in, obviously trying to keep the conversation light. "Coco was doing a miserable job on her own. Dressing up in crazy costumes, popping up every time we turned around. We had to do something just to get her off our backs."

"Okay, back to the original subject, Blue. No more of your distraction tactics." She turned to Toni. "The point is, it's good to finally see Blue settle down. Last time I saw him in action—"

"Hey, two can play this game, Ms. Coco," Blue interrupted. "Last time I saw *you* in action, you were setting off to teach old big foot over there how to do the Macarena. You owe me twenty bucks if you weren't successful."

Jax, who was still leaning against the bar, ankles crossed and holding a wineglass in one hand, the epitome of sophistication, chose this moment to enter the fray. "I do not dance. Is that clear? I *will* not dance. Not even here."

Coco giggled. "We get it . . . You will not dance in a bar. You do not dance in the car."

"He does not dance in a club," Blue sang. "He will not dance with a shrub."

Toni couldn't resist adding the final line. "Jax will not dance, Sam I am, but how about green eggs and ham?"

Coco stretched across Blue to give Toni a high five. "Toni, that was right on cue."

Jax rolled his eyes and sipped his wine with a superior British air, but she could see he was hiding a grin behind his glass.

Apparently Blue had noticed it, too. "I see you grinning on the sly back there. You can try to pretend, but you're not fooling anyone. Your dark brooding days are over. Coco has made sure of that."

"Well, I was trying to be subtle and wait for you two to notice," Coco said. "But I can see that's not going to happen." She held out her hand and wiggled her fingers, letting the light dance on the large, square-cut diamond ring on her hand. "*Hello.* Will you look at the rock Jax gave me?"

Toni grabbed Coco's hand. "Oh my gosh. It's gorgeous."

"Well it's about damn time," Blue said, clapping Jax on the back. "So you finally made it official."

"He proposed on Valentine's Day." Coco crossed the room to cuddle up against Jax, who immediately lifted an arm to draw her against his side. "It was so romantic. Remember how mad he was at me last summer because he thought I was only interested in drama and adventure?"

Blue nodded.

"Well, he decided he was going to give me my own romantic adventure. He took me out on his estate in Massachusetts, which was covered with a foot and a half of snow. Then he insisted that we build a snowman in one particular spot."

"You're kidding," Blue said. "This man actually suggested you play in the snow?"

"Yes. He'd buried the ring, and then waited for me to find it. I have to tell you, though, I almost missed it because I wasn't really in the mood to linger out there. It was freezing. My heart wasn't in it, and I hadn't been paying attention."

"She would have buried the ring in the snowman's head, if I hadn't shouted, 'Hey, what's that there?' just in time," Jax said.

"After I realized what it was and took it out of the box, he got down on one knee—in the snow—and proposed. I accepted, of course. Then, after that . . . well, let's just say I've come to appreciate *playing* in the snow a lot more."

Jax seemed a bit embarrassed and cleared his throat. "We decided to drop by uninvited, Blue, because I want to ask you an important favor. Obviously, as my only friend, as you put it, I would like you to be my best man."

Blue grinned devilishly, squinting at his watch. "Uh,

I don't know. Let me check my schedule. Just kidding."
Blue reached out and hugged Coco and Jax. "Of course.
I'd be honored. I'm really happy for you. I knew the
first time I saw you two together that you were perfect
for each other."

Toni gave the couple her congratulations, as well. It
felt good to see two people so obviously in love with each
other. But what really affected her was Blue's reaction to
the news.

It may have been paranoia, but Toni would have
argued that Blue was already looking at *her* differently.
Every so often, when she looked up and found his eyes
on her he seemed to be studying her. Sizing her up.
Measuring her. Lord save them both if it were for a
wedding gown.

There was a knock at the door and Blue went to
answer it, letting in the delivery man who'd brought
the dinner he'd ordered from the restaurant down the
street. After arranging covered plates on the table, Blue
sat next to Toni on the sofa. Coco and Jax sat across
from them in chairs.

The Cajun shrimp and crab cakes were delicious, but
Toni was finding it difficult to concentrate on her food.
Blue stayed close and was constantly touching her, pat-
ting her leg, brushing her arm, or squeezing her thigh.
Normally she enjoyed his touch, but she was suddenly
feeling cramped. To make matters worse, he kept asking
Jax and Coco to discuss their wedding plans. Will it
be a church wedding? Formal or informal? How many
guests?

It wasn't that she wasn't interested. It was just that
Blue's eagerness was beginning to make her uncomfort-
able. Finally, Toni just couldn't take it anymore.
"Excuse me." She stood, heading for Blue's private
restroom.

Blue looked up, giving her an apologetic smile. "The sink in my bathroom is broken. There's another one that the staff uses at the bottom of the stairs."

"I'll come with you," Coco said, getting up to follow her.

Toni tried not to gnash her teeth. She knew the other woman was only being friendly, but she desperately needed a moment to herself. Still, she waited at the door for Coco to catch up with her.

When she met Coco at the bathroom counter later, Toni prepared herself to make light conversation. "So how long have you—"

"It was getting pretty rough in there, wasn't it?" Coco said, leveling Toni with her smoky gaze.

Toni's lips parted. "What?"

"It's okay." Coco reached out and touched her arm. "I could see the expression on your face. It was as though Blue had been kidnapped by aliens who left a mushy, love-struck, groomsman in his place."

She sighed with relief. "Oh, so you noticed it, too."

Coco gracefully eased onto the countertop to look down at Toni. "He's got it bad for you, honey. It's true I haven't known him long, but I've never seen Blue this way. He was always too busy playing the role of a ladies' man."

Toni nodded. Just as she'd suspected. To a sexy, blue-eyed nightclub owner, womanizing was inevitable. Then again, she'd dated undercover players before. Blue never received mysterious phone calls in the middle of the night. They'd spent many evenings surrounded by beautiful women, and his eyes never strayed. Toni always received his full attention. For a known tomcat, Blue sure didn't behave like one.

"Of course, it's just that," Coco continued. "An act. Men like Blue and Jax don't fall in love easily, but

when they do, it's serious. Jax tried to protect himself
by freezing everyone out. I think Blue's defense mecha-
nism is the appearance of letting *everyone* in. I've got a
feeling Toni, that it's the real thing with you."

Toni inhaled deeply. This conversation should have
made her uncomfortable, but Coco was open and direct,
making it surprisingly easy to talk to her.

"Blue and I haven't really talked about our feelings
for each other yet. I know it's turning into something
serious, which is great, but . . ."

"It's kinda scary," Coco finished for her.

"Exactly. There's just no way to be sure."

Coco threw back her head and laughed. "If you're
waiting to be sure, give up right now. There's no such
thing. Sometimes you just have to go with what you
know in your heart."

Before Toni could respond, Coco gave her a self-
deprecating smile. "I know, cornball city, right? Straight
off a T.V. sitcom. What can I tell you? I'm an actress,
and I practically grew up in front of the television."

"I understand what you're saying. It's just that all of
a sudden Blue has gotten so . . ."

Coco waved her off. "I know. It's the way their minds
work. Jax spent the entire summer running away from
what was happening between us. When he finally came
to terms with it he kidnapped me from my apartment.
At first he was so overprotective and . . . well, clingy. It
was difficult for him to believe I wasn't going to disap-
pear. But eventually he began to relax and trust that
what we have is strong and lasting. You just have to wait
it out."

Toni nodded, keeping silent. Most women had the
opposite problem. They had men who *feared* commit-
ment. Blue had never hidden his feelings for her. He

hadn't said he loved her yet, but she sensed that was because he knew she wasn't ready to deal with it.

Coco slipped off the counter. "Look, I'm not trying to make you feel more pressured. I just wanted to put in a good word for Blue, before he completely blows it. He and Jax are a lot alike."

Toni laughed. "You're kidding." She hadn't known Jax long, but he had tall, dark, and brooding written all over him. Blue's personality was open and friendly. If Blue were the sun, Jax would be the moon.

"I know what you're thinking, but it's true. Obviously they complement each other—Jax keeps Blue grounded, and Blue keeps Jax from taking himself too seriously. But they also relate to each other like no one else can. According to Jax, Blue has a dark side. I've never actually seen it, but I know he's right. With the kind of pasts the two of them share, they can't help but take a little of that inside themselves. You know what I mean?"

"Yeah. Sure," Toni said, though of course she hadn't a clue. *Dark side.* Blue? Just what kind of past did he share with Jax?

Coco looked at her watch. "Whoa, if we don't get back, we're in for an entire evening of jokes about women who go to the ladies' room together."

Toni automatically followed Coco from the bathroom. She was still mulling over their conversation. This was the point at which she'd normally let her heart explain away all her doubts and apprehensions, but this time Toni had promised herself that she'd be smarter. She couldn't ignore it.

The warning signs were beginning to surface.

CHAPTER NINE

Toni stomped down on the gas pedal of her little convertible. She was already fifteen minutes late meeting Blue and his friends at the restaurant. Jax and Coco would be getting on an airplane tomorrow morning, and after that she and Blue were going to have a little talk.

Rolling her eyes, Toni slammed on the brakes as she got caught at the light just outside Coffee.com's parking lot. Sighing heavily, she looked around. She was still twenty minutes away from the restaurant. She looked around, impatiently tapping her fingers on the door frame. A familiar figure caught her eye.

One of the men who had chased her two nights ago was crossing the street toward her. Okay, this wasn't a coincidence. It was creepy. Obviously he'd been waiting for her. She looked to the right and saw another man crossing toward her from the other side. Was she crazy, or did this one look just like the other?

They were weaving through traffic, and it didn't take a genius to see that she was their target. Toni looked up at the light. It was still red, allowing traffic coming from the opposite direction to turn in front of her lane.

Feeling a drop of perspiration trickle down her back, she watched the men move in on her. Her chest constricted as she eased down on the gas pedal. She was the first car at the light. Mentally she willed red to turn green.

The man on her left was coming closer to her driver's side door. Her car was open, and they would easily be able to climb inside. She couldn't let that happen.

As she rammed her foot onto the gas pedal, her convertible shot forward into the intersection. She cut off a little Suzuki jeep, but she managed to make it through the red light without causing an accident.

Without easing up on the gas pedal she looked into her rearview mirror. Apparently the light had finally turned green, and the two men were caught in the street, blocking traffic. Toni sped up, the drumming of her heartbeat drowning out the honking horns behind her.

"Here she comes now," Blue said with relief when he finally saw Toni's harried face as she strode through the restaurant toward them. He stood, pulling out her chair as she neared the table. "There you are, honey. We were beginning to get a little worried."

Toni sat down and took a deep breath. "Hi. Sorry I'm late. I got delayed at the shop."

"Don't worry about it. We understand." Coco touched Toni's arm. "When you run your own business it's hard to keep nine to five hours. Help yourself to some crab dip."

"No, thanks," Toni said with a tight smile. Her hands were shaking as she unfolded her napkin and spread it in her lap.

Blue leaned toward her. "Are you all right?"

She reached out and took a sip of her water. "I'm fine. I had to rush because April showed up late for her shift, and traffic was . . . hectic on the way over."

Blue nodded, but he could tell that she was more fidgety than usual. He rubbed her back to soothe her. "We haven't ordered yet. The food here is fantastic, so I hope you're hungry."

Toni picked up her menu and quickly made a selection. When the waiter came for their orders, Toni ordered a gin and tonic with her meal. Blue's eyebrows rose. He'd never seen Toni drink during dinner unless it was a special occasion.

Coco leaned toward Toni. "Tell us about Coffee.com. Blue says it's an Internet café. I've always been intrigued by those."

"Yes. We've been open for a little over a month, and it seems to be doing really well."

Blue listened while Toni talked about the café. Her body had relaxed a bit, but he could sense that something was wrong. He didn't know what had happened, but he was beginning to worry. Experience had taught him that there was no such thing as a coincidence, and Toni had been surrounded by a lot of them lately. First her home had been burglarized, and then she was chased through her condo complex by two thugs.

He didn't feel Toni was safe where she was living, and he intended to tell her so that night. Being around Coco and Jax had affected him more strongly than he'd realized. Seeing the so happy together and planning for their wedding had only reminded him of how much he wanted those things.

Toni was still a little shy when it came to discussing their feelings for each other, but he knew she loved him even though she hadn't said so. She wasn't the kind of woman who took relationships casually. That much he knew. Everyone had battle wounds from past relationships that made them a little wary of love, but he knew Toni hadn't been through anything a few Band-Aids and his love couldn't fix. She didn't realize it, but Toni had healing powers of her own. When she was around, he didn't have to work so hard to keep his demons at bay. Her easy laughter, sultry kisses, and natural sweetness were the light that chased his shadows away.

The waiter brought their dinners, and Toni seemed to have relaxed a bit more. She and Coco were chatting like old friends.

"Have you decided where you'll go for your honeymoon yet?" Toni asked.

"Yes and no," Coco said, picking a red pepper out of her salad with her fingers and biting into it. "Believe it or not, last summer sort of dulled my desire to travel for a while."

Blue snorted in surprise.

Coco glared at him. "I know traveling from Philly to Florida in five weeks isn't exactly world travel, but it satisfied my wanderlust for the time being."

"And I suppose Jax satisfies all your other lusts these days," Blue quipped.

"Ignore him." Toni rolled her eyes at Blue. "Does this mean you've decided not to go away for your honeymoon?"

"Not exactly. In case you missed the accent, Jax is from London, and we've kicked around the idea of spending a few weeks there."

"Oh, that sounds wonderful. Jax, do you have family in London?"

Jax shook his head. "I'm afraid not." His tone seemed normal, but Blue didn't miss the icy chill that formed in Jax's eyes for just a moment. Then Jax looked over at Coco, and his warmth was restored. Blue saw them take each other's hands under the table.

If that didn't prove that love could heal all wounds, nothing did. Jax had some pretty heavy duty scars in his past. So did Blue, for that matter.

Not wanting to let his thoughts travel that path, Blue resorted to humor. "What's the point of spending money on an expensive honeymoon vacation when everyone knows you're going to spend the entire time inside one room?"

Coco winked at Toni. "The point is, when you finally come up for air you want to be able to look out the window and see an interesting view."

"Enough of your churlishness, Blue," Jax said with his aristocratic accent. "There are ladies present. Act as if you have some couth."

Toni grinned. "The act would be wasted. I think Coco and I both know that he doesn't."

Coco laughed. "Yes. I got to see Blue's true colors last summer."

"Hey." Blue tried to make a token protest. "Being cooped up in a stuffy tour bus in the middle of June can bring out the worst in a person. You owe me big for that one, Jax."

Jax arched his eyebrow. "Pssh. True, you did me a favor last summer, but that goes both ways. I've pulled your sorry arse out of a few fires myself."

Blue tried to make light of it, not wanting Toni to get the wrong impression. "Come on, Jax. Covering for me when those Mary Kay reps got out of hand doesn't count.''

''Do I have to remind you of Mexico? If I hadn't pulled you out of that freezer when I did, you never would have gotten—''

''All's fair in love and war.'' Blue made a completely irrelevant statement, hoping to distract Toni from what Jax had been about to say. At the same time he shot Jax a warning look. ''Anyone up for dessert?''

Before they left the restaurant, Jax pulled Blue aside while the women were in the ladies' room.

''What was all that about at dinner?''

Blue shrugged. ''What do you mean?''

Jax leaned against the wall, regarding his friend carefully. ''The hush hush at the table. Haven't you discussed your past with Toni?''

''No, I haven't. There hasn't been a reason to get in to all that with her.''

Wrinkles creased Jax's forehead. ''What do you mean, there hasn't been a reason? It seems pretty clear that you're serious about the young woman.''

''Yeah. So?'' Blue said, deliberately being difficult.

''Ahh, this is refreshing. Last summer I had to endure your tiresome ribbing over my feelings for Coco. You watched me suffer and had a good laugh, while I stubbornly refused to admit what was happening. I didn't anticipate getting to return the favor so soon.''

Now Blue was confused. ''Unlike you, I'm not running away from my feelings for Toni. Quite the opposite.''

''That's what you think. I know what's going through your head. You're thinking if you don't tell her about your past, you can shield her from the ugliness you've encountered.''

"What Toni and I have is very special. When we're together, it's magic. There's no need to—"

"Now that's where you're wrong. If you love her, eventually you'll have to tell her everything. Love is all consuming. And you can't really live in it until you've shone light on all the dark corners of your soul. If she loves you in return, she won't be frightened away. I learned that the hard way with Coco."

"Things are different with you and Coco. She didn't wait for you to come for her. Coco came to you. Toni's different. I don't think she's ready—"

"Obviously, neither are you if you aren't ready to share all of yourself—the light *and* the dark." Blue tried to interrupt, but Jax wouldn't let him. "Fine. I'll say nothing more. Just as you did, I'll just sit back and wait for you to come to your senses. I'm sorry I won't be around to see how this one turns out. I would enjoy watching you squirm a little."

Blue just stood there staring at his longtime friend as if he'd never seen him before. "I don't think I like you this way. When you decide to go back to brooding and being grim, let me know."

Jax threw his head back and laughed heartily—something that Blue had never seen from his friend, before Coco.

"Okay, but just one drink," Toni said stubbornly as she walked into Blue's home. "I really can't stay tonight. I'm working tomorrow morning."

"That's fine. I just think we should talk."

She'd been thinking the same thing. She just didn't know where to begin—with her run-in with those two men on the road, or with Blue's mysterious past.

He walked over to the bar and poured her a brandy,

taking a Yoo-hoo for himself. He handed her the drink and sat down on the sofa beside her. "I saw the way you looked when you got to the restaurant tonight. Is everything okay?"

Toni took a deep breath, staring into the bottom of her glass. She'd been hoping to work up to this a bit more. She knew he was going to be upset and would worry. In fact, she was pretty worried herself.

"Actually, something did happen," she said slowly.

Blue put his drink down and turned to face her. "What is it?"

"I saw those two men again. The ones who chased me in the parking lot."

"Where? When did this happen?"

"I was in my car. I'd just left the cafe and had stopped at a light. Next thing I knew they were coming at me from both sides. They must have been waiting for me to leave."

"Coming at you from both sides?" Blue asked, sounding confused. "Were they in cars?"

"No. They were on foot. I drove out of the lot and got caught at the light. I saw the first one coming toward my car from across the street. The other one crossed toward me from the other side. I had the top down on my convertible. I was afraid they would jump inside."

Blue swore, rubbing his palm over his forehead. "What did you do?"

"The only thing I could think of. The light was still red, but I was the lead car, so I pulled off into the intersection."

He put his head in his hands, rubbing his eyes. "You could've been killed."

"I know, but it was a reflex. At least they didn't get to me. The light changed and they were stuck in the middle of the street. By then I was long gone."

"That's it." The determined tone of Blue's voice made Toni look up in surprise.

"This is ridiculous, and it's getting out of hand. I should have done something two days ago when those punks tried to corner you in the parking lot."

"Blue, what could you have done? We don't even know—"

"You're moving in with me. You're not safe where you are, and that's the only way I can protect you. This has gone on too long already."

"Wait a minute—"

Blue wasn't listening. He'd gotten to his feet and was crossing to the telephone. He'd picked it up and had started dialing before he realized Toni was calling his name.

He paused with the phone in his hand. "What is it?"

Toni shook her head in frustration. She couldn't believe her easygoing, laid back Blue was acting like a dictator. "What are you doing?"

"I'm getting ready to call the police."

"Slow down. For starters, the police practically blew me off last time. You said yourself that they weren't going to be very helpful. Second, I can't move in with you."

Blue sighed, hanging up the phone.

"Look, we're going to play by the rules and make all the reports. I'll take care of the rest. Now as for moving in with me ... sweetheart, I know I didn't ask you in the most romantic way, but—"

Toni got to her feet to look him in the eye.

"You didn't ask me at all. You insisted. How can you just *decide* something that affects both of our futures like that?"

He walked around the couch, sat down, and pulled her down beside him. "You're right. I shouldn't have said it the way I did. But I think it's something we should talk about. This is serious, Toni. These incidents are happening too frequently to be coincidences. Did you recognize these two men?''

"I definitely recognized one of those guys from the parking lot the other night. I don't know if I've ever seen him before that."

"What about the other one?"

"Well, that's easy. He looked just like the other one. Get this. They're twins."

"Twins? Identical?"

She nodded.

"Believe it or not, that might make things easier for us. How were they dressed?"

Toni shrugged. "Like normal guys around that age, I guess."

"What age?"

"Early twenties. They wore jeans. Tommy Hilfiger shirts. Nothing unusual."

"This is only the second time you've seen these two?"

"As far as I know."

Blue shook his head, obviously deep in thought. "We need to find out if the police followed up with your neighbors. We might be able to get some answers right now." He went back to the phone and dialed the local police station.

Toni was startled by the grave set of his features. Blue was always smiling and upbeat. He was the first one to crack jokes to lighten the mood whenever things got too heavy. The last time she'd been in a tight spot, he'd just held her close and soothed her with his calming voice.

The Blue she saw now was shades darker than the

Blue she was used to. Her Blue was a bright turquoise, like the water in his pool outside—cool and inviting, translucent in the light. This Blue was deep midnight, like an ocean at dark—shadowy and intense, with hidden depths.

"What did they say?" she asked when he hung up the phone.

"Same old story. They'll check into it and get back to us. I doubt they'll get to it. I talked to an old buddy of mine. All their resources are being poured into some big narcotics homicide involving a visiting politician." Blue swore again. "Tomorrow, after I drive Jax and Coco to the airport, we'll question your neighbors ourselves."

Toni wanted to protest, but it actually was a comfort to have him take charge this way. The fact was, she didn't have the first clue where to go from here.

"Can you think of any reason why these two kids would be after you? Anything they might want from you?"

"April and I have only been here for a few months. I don't know anyone here."

"Do you think April might know them?"

"That's a good question. I doubt it, but I'll have to ask her."

"There has to be some connection. This isn't a random stalking. These men want something from you."

"Money? If that's what they're after, they're bound to be disappointed. We sank our lottery winnings into the business. Now we're back to living on a budget just like everyone else."

"I doubt it's just money. If that was what they were after, they would have taken it when they broke into your house."

"So you *do* think they were the same men."

"It's a logical conclusion. That's why I really think it would be best if you moved in with me until we figure this out."

"I can't move in with you," Toni said quickly.

"Why not?"

"Why not? Well . . . what about April? If it's not safe there, I can't just leave her there."

"It seems pretty obvious that these two punks are interested in you, not April. Nevertheless, she's welcome to stay here, too. There's plenty of room. Although, my guess is that Marcus would prefer to be the one to put her up for a few weeks."

A few weeks? Toni couldn't handle how serious this whole situation was becoming. At first she'd thought Blue was just using the "move in with me" line to press his advantage. But if he was willing to move April in, too, he clearly thought she might be in real danger.

"Do you really think that's necessary? Maybe you and Marcus cooked up this whole scheme to force April and me into cohabitation," Toni joked, hoping to lighten the mood.

Blue just stared at her. That's when Toni knew she was losing control of the situation. Blue never passed up an opportunity for humor. On the other hand, how much did she really know about this man? Here he was asking her to put her life in his hands for the next few weeks, and she hadn't known anything about him two months ago.

"You know I'm not joking, Toni. This is serious. I want you to move in with me because I love you, but I know you aren't ready for that kind of a commitment. Right now I'm asking you to move in because I can keep you safer here."

Toni sat staring back at him. "You love me?"

For the first time in what seemed like hours, Blue smiled. "You already knew that. Let's not play games, Toni. We both know what we have here. If you're honest with yourself, you'll see it."

Toni found herself getting angry. She knew it was irrational, but she hated the fact that he could look into her soul and state her most intimate thoughts as though it were no big deal.

Yes. She'd known he loved her. Toni loved him, too. If she went with her heart, Blue was everything she'd ever wanted, and more, but it wasn't that simple.

"I'm not playing games, Blue," she said through clenched teeth."

"Then tell me the truth. What are your feelings for me?"

"Tell you the *truth*? I haven't been lying to you."

"No, you've just carefully avoided discussing your feelings." He reached out and took her by the shoulders. "This is True Blue you're talking to. I'm a human lie detector. Care to take the test?"

Toni felt the overwhelming urge to look away from his penetrating blue gaze. She forced herself not to. "I don't know what you're talking about."

"You said you're not playing games. That you're not hiding from your feelings for me. If that's true, let's put it to the test."

Unwilling to back down, Toni had to go along. "Fine. Fire away."

He moved close to her so they were sitting shoulder to shoulder. Then he took her hands in his. He looked deeply into her eyes. "Are you ready?"

She wasn't, but it was too late to turn back now. "Yeah. Go for it."

"Is your name Antoinette Rivers?"

Rolling her eyes, she said, "Yes."

"Good. Now, do you have a sister named Broom-hilda?"

"No," she said, feeling her jaw stiffen. Why was she letting him do this? It was a waste of time.

"Good. Are you in love with Blue Cooper?"

Toni opened her mouth, wanting to say no. "Yes."

"*Very* good." His eyes were flashing with mischief. "Is Blue Cooper the best lover you've ever been with?"

A hot blush stole over her cheeks. "Yes."

"Great." Blue was smiling uncontrollably now. "Do you want to move in with Blue Cooper?"

Finally, a question Toni *wanted* to answer. "No. I don't," she answered emphatically.

His eyebrows rose in surprise. His grip on her hands relaxed. "Why not?" The indignation in his voice was unmistakable. "You just admitted that you're in love with me. I love you, too. The circumstances may not be ideal, but moving in here is the only solution that makes sense."

Toni pulled away from him and stood up. She needed to put some distance between them. "How can you talk about moving in together as if it's no big deal? There are so many things we don't know about each other." She watched him scratch his head in confusion. "Are you through with your little lie detector test? Because I have some questions of my own."

He spread his arms wide as if his life were an open book. "Go ahead. What do you want to know?"

"Well, first I'd like to know what you used to do for a living. You cut Jax off at dinner tonight when he started to talk about some adventure the two of you had gotten into. Were you a professional bodyguard? Most nightclub owners don't typically find themselves called out to moonlight on cross-country book tours."

"No one starts out as a nightclub owner," Blue said.

She folded her arms across her chest. "Well, what did *you* start out as?"

"I took a lot of odd jobs to keep the rent money flowing."

"Such as?" Toni began to have a sinking feeling in the pit of her stomach.

She'd been down this road before—too many times to count. Blue was hiding something. So much for True Blue. He put up a better front than most, but it was starting to look as if he were no better than any of the other men she'd dated.

"I have worked as a bodyguard. I've also done other types of security work. Not anything for you to get bent out of shape about. Last summer I was just doing a favor for a friend. Nothing more."

"Nothing more? True Blue, can you look me in the eyes and tell me that there's nothing about your past that you're keeping from me?"

He sighed deeply, and Toni could feel the air in the room go still. "Toni . . . my past is complicated."

"Is that your way of telling me that you don't want to talk about it?"

He looked up at her, his expression carved from stone. "You know, I really *don't* want to talk about it. In fact, I spend a lot of time trying not to even think about it."

He stood up, walking over to the bar for another drink. "It doesn't have anything to do with us. There's nothing that went on in my past that can change what we have. That should be enough for you."

Her gaze bored a hole in his back. "What if it isn't?"

"Then I'd have to ask you why." He walked back over to her to look her in the eyes. "Why is it so hard for you to trust me? Have I ever lied to you?"

She returned his gaze just as boldly. "I don't know, have you?"

Toni watched his face. Those warm, liquid blue eyes froze over like a winter lake. She knew she'd insulted him, but she didn't understand why he wouldn't confide in her. Here he wanted her to move her life into his, but he didn't want to share his past with her? How could he expect unconditional trust if he weren't able to give the same?

"Are you serious?" Blue's voice was low. He spoke very slowly. "In all this time we've spent together, you're still not sure if you can trust me?"

She started to answer him, but he wasn't finished.

"All the talks we've had. All the times you needed something, and I was there for you. None of that counts for anything? You still think you need *proof* of who I am?"

"It's not that—"

"I know you're distrustful of men, but I've gone out of my way to show you where my heart is. If you're still not convinced, then there's nothing I can tell you that will change that."

For an instant, Toni felt as though her heart had stopped beating. The look in his eyes made her feel miserable for causing him to look at her that way. She knew they'd come to a critical point in their relationship.

"What are you saying?" she asked cautiously.

"I'm saying that you're right. We probably aren't ready to have this conversation. Why don't you take some time to really think about what it is that you want?"

"A few days?"

He nodded and then turned away from her.

Toni felt as though she'd been dismissed. Without another word she picked up her purse and left.

CHAPTER TEN

Monday evening Toni sat slumped in front of the television set. She'd been there since she'd left Coffee.com that afternoon, and she didn't see herself moving anytime soon.

She was probably in a state of shock from the argument she and Blue had last night. Once again she'd gotten what she'd gone after, and once again she didn't want it now that she had it.

Hurting Blue was the last thing she'd wanted to do, but she really hadn't considered the possibility. For all this time, she'd been thinking only of her *own* feelings. Because of her attitude toward men and her lack of trust, she'd let what she'd been trying to prevent from happening to herself happen to Blue.

A ridiculous cartoon drama was playing on television, but Toni couldn't see it. All she could see was the look in Blue's eyes before she'd left him last night. She'd blown it. Once and for all. Toni had proven that she wasn't meant to be happy.

Time came and went as Toni sat, absently staring at the television screen, mentally replaying her conversation with Blue. That was where April found her when she got home that evening.

"Hey, Sis. What's on?"

Toni shrugged.

"Well, we had a good night at the café. While I was surfing the net, I found the perfect card for Marcus online. I E-mailed it to him. I hope he's gotten it by now." April put something in front of Toni's face. "Look, I printed it out so you could see it. It expressed exactly how I feel about him."

Toni took the card and scanned the front quickly. The mushy sentiment only made her angry. She tossed the printout onto the coffee table. "You aren't supposed to be surfing the Internet while you're working. You should be managing the business. Making phone calls, going over the books, checking on supplies. When all of that's done, you can help the waitresses at the front counter."

"Well, excuse the hell out of me, but I was doing all of those things. Forgive me, but, I thought when I hired the staff I was looking for people who were actually competent enough to do their jobs by themselves."

April leaned forward, hands on hips. "Natalie is a great assistant manager, and the waitstaff is quite capable. So after I did the office work and checked on the staff, I decided to do a little product testing!" April ended her last sentence screaming at the top of her lungs.

Still self-absorbed, Toni just rolled her eyes. "What's wrong with you?"

"What's wrong with *me*? I'm not the one walking

around here like Miss PMS of nineteen ninety-nine. I don't change moods with the wind, lecture at will, and mope even when things are going well."

Toni blinked. She *had* been acting that way. Great. Now it wasn't just Blue who hated her, she'd alienated her own sister, as well. Feeling lower than ever, a muttered "I'm sorry," was all she could manage.

April sat down beside her. "Look, I know you've been shaken up lately, ever since those thugs chased you around the block, but—"

"That isn't all that's happened. I think those are the same guys who broke in here, and for all I know they may have been trying to carjack me when they approached me outside the café yesterday."

"Carjack you? What are you talking about?"

Toni quickly recounted her run-in with the twins the day before.

"Okay, this is getting creepy. You don't have any idea who these guys could be, and why they'd be after you?"

"No, I don't. I was hoping something might ring a bell with you."

"Nope. I arrived at this party the same time you did. I don't know anyone in Florida."

"Could there be anyone who might have followed you from D.C.?"

"I know you think I've had a lot of boyfriends, but I really haven't—"

"That's not what I'm saying. I'm just asking a simple question. I've wracked my brain, and I can't figure out what they'd be after. It can't be the money, because we declined to do any publicity for our lottery win for just that reason. No one else should know about it. Right? Did *you* tell anyone?"

April chewed on her lower lip.

"Did you, April?"

"No, I didn't tell anyone that we won the lottery. What does Blue think about all this?"

"He freaked out. He wanted me to move in with him until we figure out what's going on."

"That sounds like a good idea."

"I said he *wanted* me to move in. He doesn't anymore."

April made herself comfortable beside her. "What happened?"

"We had an argument. I didn't think I should stay with him, even for a short time. There are too many things I don't know about him. His past is so—"

"I knew it," April said, rolling her eyes.

"What exactly did you think you knew?"

"I knew you weren't going to be able to handle the whole concept of an affair. I knew you were too much of a prude to carry it off."

"How can you say that? The fact that I even considered it shows I'm not a prude." Toni turned sideways and gave her sister her full attention. "I don't know why you ever thought I was."

She shook her head when April regarded her skeptically. What had she done to make anyone think her "prudish"? She couldn't remember ever behaving that way. Quite the opposite, in fact. "You and I aren't that different."

Her eyes scanned her sister. April was wearing a sexy, white halter top and black leather pants. She looked down at her own clothing. She wore a plain white T-shirt with cuffed sleeves and a pair of black jeans.

Okay, outwardly Toni was clearly the more conservative of the two, but that didn't make her prudish. She pinned April with her gaze. "One of us has to be responsible, and I'm the oldest. That doesn't automatically mean I'm uptight or repressed."

April crossed her arms over her chest. "What are you talking about? I'm responsible . . . I just like to have fun, too."

"I like to have fun, too. Why is that such a surprise?" Toni knew she was getting defensive, but April had struck a nerve. "I guess when you and I are in the same room your antics draw everyone's attention. When they finally get to know me, they're amazed to discover that I'm not some huge stick in the mud."

April waved her off. "Don't exaggerate. No one thinks you're a stick in the mud. But everyone knows I'm the hell-raiser and you're the sophisticated one. It's always been that way."

Toni shook her head. It hadn't always been that way. Over the years she'd been subtly changing. Before they moved to Florida, she'd taken a good look at herself. She'd been afraid she'd wake up one morning and find that she'd turned into their mother. That, combined with what Jordan Banks put her through, had sent her spinning. She'd managed to convince herself that she could protect her heart if she looked for a fling instead of romance.

She'd been on this kind of inevitable collision course before—years ago. She could blame that foolishness on youth.

"Do you remember what I was like in high school?"

"Of course." April wrinkled her nose. "Valedictorian. Rub it in."

"I'm not talking about that. My freshman year? You don't remember?"

April frowned, shaking her head. "When you were a freshman, I was . . . I don't know, ten or eleven? What are you getting at?"

Toni raised her eyebrows. She wasn't sure why it was suddenly so important that her sister remember one of the most difficult times in her life, but for some reason it was. "I guess Mom and Dad kept it quiet. I always thought you knew."

"What? Tell me." April folded her legs beneath her, cuddling a throw pillow.

Toni leaned back against the cushions. "Do you remember when I was dating Rick Tyler?" April shook her head. "He was a senior. Popular and cute. I was so flattered that he wanted to date me. He took me to all the parties and football games. We had a good time together."

"It's coming back to me," April said, nodding. "That's when Mom and Dad were yelling at you all the time for staying out late."

Toni nodded. The memories were as clear as they would have been if they'd happened yesterday. "They said I wasn't concentrating on school, and they were right. Whenever one of them dropped me off at the library, Rick would pick me up and take me to the movies or the mall."

April's face lit with devilish glee. "Ahh, so you weren't such a good girl, after all. How come I missed all this?"

Toni continued as though April hadn't spoken. It still hurt to think of the mistakes she'd made. "One night after a football game, Rick took me to his grandparents' place. They were on vacation, and he had a key so he could feed their cats."

April's eyebrows lifted. "Oh?"

Toni stared at her feet propped on the coffee table. "I didn't come home until almost three A.M. that morning." She met her sister's eyes. "I lost my virginity that night, April, and it was horrible. Not what I'd expected at all. I ended up feeling so . . . disappointed."

"Oh no. I had no idea." April leaned forward to squeeze Toni's hand, then sank back against the cushions, shaking her head. "I always thought that guy you dated in college was your first."

"You thought that because that's what I wanted you to think. When I got home that night Mom and Dad were waiting up for me. I'm not sure if they knew what had happened, but they really let me have it. They told me I was trying to grow up too fast. They said I had to start thinking about what I was doing, set a better example for you. Act more responsibly."

"Whoa. I guess you took that advice to heart."

"Not right away. It didn't help that Rick didn't have much to say to me after I'd slept with him. He had plenty to say to his friends. He told them everything. After that I became very popular with the guys."

Toni felt a stinging heat creeping up her cheeks. "I couldn't handle it. I had to turn things around so I wouldn't spend my high school career marked as a slut."

"You?" April's eyes were wide. "Are you kidding me?"

"No. I'm not. Even though Rick was the only guy I was with until I met Derek at Howard, I didn't completely live down my reputation until my junior year."

April nodded. "That explains those daily lectures you gave me when I entered high school. I just thought you were being a pain."

Toni shook her head. "Unfortunately, I've learned all my lessons the hard way."

April was silent for a while, then she looked up and gave Toni a serious look. "So what are you saying? These past few years as a good girl were a routine? You've just reverted to form in the last couple of months?"

"No. I'm just saying we're not all that different. It's just that following your impulses works for you, April. But when I do it everything gets messed up. Take this whole mess with Blue. I really thought that I could keep things from getting out of control between us."

April leaned over and put her arm around Toni. "You don't know what a relief it is to hear that you're not perfect. Especially when it comes to relationships. I was beginning to wonder if there was something wrong with *me*."

Toni looked up in surprise. "What are you talking about? You breeze through life by the seat of your pants, and somehow everything just magically works out. When I plan things and do everything by the book, things don't work out. When I decide to be impulsive and fly by the seat of my pants, that doesn't work out, either. I just can't win."

"That's not true. This thing with Blue is only messing with your head because it's the real thing and you don't know how to handle it."

"How do you know it's the real thing?"

"Because that's how I feel about Marcus. And before your thoughts get carried away, he and I haven't slept together."

Toni studied April. "Are you serious?"

"Yes. I've never been in love before. I wasn't even sure if love existed, but since I met Marcus my whole perspective has changed."

Toni pulled her fingers through her hair. "Well, how come it was so easy for you to adjust to it when I still can't get a grip on it?"

"Because you've spent your whole life looking for real love, and have only found disappointment. You finally gave up and decided it didn't exist. I never really looked for love, so when I found it it was a pleasant surprise. Now you're not sure what to believe. You've read so many books that you're convinced it's got to be this way or that way, instead of accepting it for what it is."

Toni reached up to massage her temples with her fingers. After a few minutes of thinking that over, she looked up at her sister. "I think you're right. Thanks, April."

"Anytime," April said, bouncing on the sofa. "It's kind of fun to play the big sister every now and then."

"You're good at it. Next time I fall off the deep end, you've got the job of talking me back to safety."

Toni pulled her sister into a hug. She was glad they'd had the chance to talk. Now she had a new understanding of April, and she felt that April probably understood her a little better, too.

It had also given her a lot to think about. But first, there was something she had to do.

Blue lay in bed that night, thinking about Toni. She'd been on his mind every second since she'd walked out of his apartment the night before. He couldn't stop thinking about how he'd blown things between them.

All he'd had to do was tell her. He wouldn't even have needed to go into detail. A rough outline of what he used to do would have been enough.

He was True Blue. He believed in honesty. Not talking about his past—not letting anyone in—was a habit that died hard. But he *did* want to tell her. He *did* want to let Toni in. That wasn't the reason he'd refused to explain. He'd shut down and backed away because Toni didn't trust him.

That was a completely new experience for Blue. Everyone close to him trusted him—they'd had to. Sometimes their lives had depended on it.

Even strangers, people he met at the club or on vacation, would tell him—after only knowing him for a few hours—that they trusted him. Blue had worked hard to earn that trust. He always played it straight. He always kept his word. He always meant what he said. That was usually enough for most people. It hadn't been enough for Toni.

The phone startled Blue out of his thoughts. "True Blue. What can I do for you?"

"Blue, it's Toni."

He was surprised by the amount of relief he felt at hearing her voice. All day he'd wanted to call, but he hadn't felt there was anything left for him to say. "How are you?"

"Well, as I'm sure you can guess, I'm not doing very well. I feel terrible about what happened between us last night. I was hoping we could talk. Can I see you tomorrow?"

"I do think we should talk, but I have to go out of town for a couple of days."

Another friend in need. Normally, he didn't have much of a life to interrupt when these last minute distress calls came in and he had to fly off to South Africa or Guam. This time Blue couldn't help cursing the timing.

"When will you be back?"

"I'm not sure. I have to help out a couple of friends. I don't know how long they're going to need me, but I'll be back as soon as I can. Can I call you?"

"Yes. Yes, please do." Her tone was both formal and dejected.

Blue wanted to reassure her somehow, but the words wouldn't come. "Okay. Take care of yourself."

He'd wanted to tell her to be careful. He'd wanted to ask if she was okay, if she'd had any other incidents with those two punks, but he was afraid of intruding. She'd effectively shut him out.

"You, too. Good-bye."

"Bye." He hung up the phone feeling slightly nauseated.

He should stay. How could he leave knowing Toni might be in danger?

On the other hand, he'd promised his friends Jaunie Douglas and Geri Treymaine that he'd be in Washington, D.C., in less than twenty-four hours. They needed his help. Toni didn't want his help. The decision was out of his hands.

April sped through the condo complex at top speed. She had a million things to do before she met Marcus for their date that night. She cursed violently when she saw a red Wrangler truck parked in her reserved space. Pulling her little Miata into the space beside it, she got out of the car and dashed for the house.

If she hurried she might have time to wash her hair and iron her purple tank dress. She let herself in, threw her purse on the sofa, and headed straight for the shower. Her fingers had just curled under her shirt to lift it over her head when she heard voices.

"I don't know where else to look, Barry. I don't see any more books."

"Check under the mattresses. Maybe it's one of those dirty books that you have to hide."

"Oh my gosh." April flattened herself against the wall. Those two punks that had been after Toni were in the house. And now she knew what they wanted.

She searched the bathroom for something to use as a weapon. At a loss for choices, she grabbed a bottle of perfume and a toilet scrubber.

"Hey Larry, did you leave the bathroom light on?"

"No. You said to leave everything just like we found it. I didn't look in the bathroom. Do you think I should? I know I like reading a good magazine when I'm on the—"

"Shut up! Someone's in there."

April knew she wouldn't get another chance. She pulled open the door and rushed into the hallway, flailing the scrubber and spraying the perfume in the eyes of the first person she saw.

"Aghhh! She got me." He went down, clutching his hands to his eyes.

The other one came running out of her bedroom and promptly tripped over his twin brother writhing on the floor. April chucked her weapons and started to run for the door. One of them grabbed her ankle, and she came crashing down.

Through the cacophony of moans and wails April heard, "My eyes! My eyes. I think I'm blind." And, "I got her. Water. Rinse out yours eyes with water."

Bodies shifted and twisted as April struggled to claw herself free, to no avail. Soon she only wrestled with one of the brothers as the blinded one extricated himself from the bottom of the heap.

"The bathroom. I can't see. Where is it?"

"Right in front of you," the other called to him.

Seconds later, April heard a loud thump as the blind one plowed into a wall. That distracted the other brother long enough for her to wriggle free, and April began to crawl toward the living room. She had almost made it over to the sofa when one of them came down on her in a tackle.

April reached out and tugged on the first thing she touched. A cord. The answering machine came off the stand and fell into her hands. Holding it with both hands, she thrust back and conked him over the head.

With a loud howl, he rolled off her, gripping his forehead in his hands.

April flipped over and sat up, just in time to see the other brother stumble out of the bathroom, red-eyed and dripping water on the carpet. He had the belt of Toni's terry cloth robe in his hands. "Hold her down. I'm going to tie her up."

"Barry! JB's going to kill us," the other one protested. Still he grabbed April's arms and pulled them behind her back.

"We can't leave her here. She's seen us, and thanks to you, *Larry*, she knows our names."

"What are we going to do?" Larry asked.

"We have to take her with us."

CHAPTER ELEVEN

Toni came home late that night feeling more exhausted than ever. She let herself into the house and headed straight for the answering machine. She didn't expect a call from Blue. He was out of town helping a friend.

Before her guilty suspicions could rise again, Toni picked up the answering machine from the floor. "Oh, April," she said with disgust. "You could have at least picked it up after you knocked it off the table."

Toni began pressing buttons and readjusting the tapes. "Great. It's broken."

Even if Blue wanted to call her, he wouldn't be able to reach her.

She turned off the lights and started down the hall toward her bedroom. April had a date with Marcus, so she knew she shouldn't expect her sister home anytime soon. "What a slob," Toni muttered, picking up her favorite perfume bottle and the toilet scrubber.

Opening the bathroom door, she rolled her eyes. Everything on the counter was soaking wet, and makeup tubes and bottles were scattered all over the sink.

"No date is so hot that you can't take a few seconds to clean up after yourself." Sighing heavily, Toni put the perfume and the scrubber down on the counter, turned off the light, and closed the door. "It must be love."

Toni slogged into her room. She missed Blue more than ever. The worst part was that she'd prepared herself to apologize, grovel, beg on bended knee—whatever it took to get him to forgive her behavior. It had taken a lot of energy for her to bury her pride, and now she hadn't even had the satisfaction of completing the job.

She didn't even know where Blue was going to be for this unspecified period of time. He said he was helping a friend. That might very well be true, but until she had the chance to talk to him, anything could happen. What if he met some gorgeous woman while he was gone?

Toni shook herself.

She trusted him. She did . . . *really*.

Blue wasn't the type of guy to be swayed by a pretty face. If he were, she'd worry about him every night when he went to work at the club. But she didn't. She knew he loved *her*.

She trusted him. She *did*. Really.

Sure, Jordan used to disappear for days at a time under the guise of "helping a friend," but Blue really *was* helping a friend. He wasn't off exploiting someone for money or orchestrating shady deals, the way Jordan had been. He was helping a friend. Whatever he'd done in his past didn't matter to her. Blue told her that himself.

And she *trusted* him. She did. Really.

* * *

"Larry, we need gas again. We've been driving for hours, and we still haven't figured a way out of this. We'd better call him."

"I don't want to call him, Barry. Let's just keep driving."

"We have to. We're running out of time."

April caught her breath as she felt the car begin to slow down. They were stopping again. Another opportunity for her to try to escape.

For the past few hours, April listened to these two dim-witted fools try to think their way out of their dilemma. She listened as they outlined their situation over and over, and when they couldn't find an answer, there was always one choice—keep driving. That had given April plenty of time to formulate a few plans of her own. It wouldn't be difficult to outsmart these two.

Larry pulled into a gas station lot and Barry took out their cellular phone. He took a long, laborious breath before he dialed. He got the infamous "him" on the phone, and at the last minute thrust the phone at Larry.

While the two of them were consumed with their loathsome task, April was working her feet out of her platform sandals. The terry cloth belt had only been a temporary binding. Once they got her out to the truck, they tied her up more tightly. Just her luck—they were both UPS workers. They gagged her mouth with cellophane packing tape and bound her wrists with thick string. She was all trussed up with nowhere to go. But April was about to change that.

Luckily, they'd left her feet unbound. She was certain that if they remained distracted long enough she could work the lock open with her toes, open the door and leap out.

Once she got into the open, someone might see her and come to her rescue. If not, she could at least run for dear life.

"Uh, no, JB, we aren't back in D.C. yet," Larry was saying. "I know, but you were so mad last time we called we thought we'd better try and correctify the situation."

April's feet were free now. Slowly she eased into a horizontal position on the seat. She extended her feet toward the door, lying still for a moment to make sure they weren't paying attention to her.

"Not exactly. We have another little problem. Barry and me kinda need your advice." Larry held the phone away from his ear.

"What's he saying?" Barry asked.

Rather than answer, Larry shoved the phone into his brother's hands. "You talk to him now."

April lifted one leg, easing her foot across the door until she felt the nub of the lock between her toes. After a few gentle tugs she was able to lift it up, unlocking it.

Barry looked over his shoulder at her and she froze. He turned back around and she dropped her foot back onto the seat, waiting for the right moment to go for the door latch.

"Slow down, JB. Just listen," Barry said. "We actually weren't doing too badly. We had a couple ideas of our own. Yeah. That's right."

April began inching her body forward on the seat, toward the door, so that once she released the latch all she'd have to do was propel herself out of the truck.

"Well, first we thought we could do like you said and just ask her where the money went. We were just going to walk up to her car and talk to her, but that didn't exactly work out. So we decided to search her place again, and that's where we ran into this little problem."

April slipped her foot under the latch and tugged it

toward her until she felt it release. Not wanting to waste a single second, she rammed both feet into the door and scooted out.

The drop was a bit bigger than she'd expected. She hit the ground hard, head first.

"Hold on, JB. The girl we kidnapped is trying to escape."

Those were the last words April heard before she lost consciousness.

Toni was pulled out of a rock solid sleep the next afternoon when the phone rang. She'd tossed and turned all night, and hadn't really fallen completely to sleep until some time around five A.M. She reached for phone, still feeling groggy. "Hello?"

"Toni? This is Natalie. We're all out of singles. I sent Stephanie to the bank once already, but now we're running low on fives, too. We need someone to get change from the safe."

She rubbed her eyes, blinking rapidly, trying to focus. "Well, can't April do that for you?"

"She's not here."

Now Toni was wide awake and livid. "What do you mean she's not there? She's doing the morning shift this week."

"That's what I thought, too. But she's not here. I halfway expected her to answer the phone. Did she oversleep?"

"That's possible. Hang tight. One of us will be down there within the hour."

"April!" Toni slammed down the phone and marched to her sister's bedroom. "April?"

Her bed hadn't been slept in. She dashed back into her bedroom and dialed Marcus's number. "Great. The line's busy. They probably had a late night and didn't bother getting up this morning.''

Toni showered and dressed quickly and drove down to the shop. She stuck around all afternoon, expecting April to come running in with profuse apologies at any moment. When she never did, Toni began to worry.

She left several messages on Marcus's machine, but he never called her back. Finally, Toni left Coffee.com to check the house again. There was still no sign of April.

When evening began to give way to the night, Toni set out looking for April. The youth center where Marcus worked was closed by the time she got there. None of April's friends had heard from her. Toni was especially frustrated by the fact that she couldn't get in touch with Marcus.

Terrible thoughts began to spin in Toni's head. At a loss for places to look, she drove to Blue Paradise. Trying to keep calm, she consoled herself with the idea that Marcus and April had decided to blow off the day's work and were now dancing, carefree, at the club.

Toni doubted that was possible. Despite giving April a hard time about it, Toni knew her sister wasn't irresponsible. She took Coffee.com seriously. Although she sometimes showed up late, forgot to order supplies, or mixed up a customer's order, April worked hard. She always had. She wouldn't disappear without warning.

Not unless something was very wrong.

Blinding pain streaked through April's head as her eyelids creaked open. She had no idea where she was. All she knew was that everything hurt.

She blinked, trying to clear her blurred vision. Moaning, April realized that her lips felt itchy and dry. She ran her fingers over them, remembering that they'd been covered with packing tape. Now they weren't. Had she been rescued?

"Larry, come here. She's waking up."

"Oh no," April said, groaning loudly. Wherever she was, the bumbling brothers were there, too.

"Finally. I thought she might have been in a coma."

"She wasn't in a coma, you idiot. She was just sleeping. Hard."

April lifted her head and tried to look around. Suddenly a large head loomed into her field of vision. She gasped and flopped back onto the pillows.

"Are you okay?"

She gripped her throbbing head. "I will be once you get your foul-smelling breath out of my face."

That sent the other one into a giggling fit. "She sure told you, Barry."

Barry covered his mouth with his hand. "I was eating corn chips."

April attempted sitting up one more time. She managed to prop a pillow behind her head and lean in a semi-upright position. Now she could see that she was in a small, two-room shack. It was too dark for her to see outside, but judging by the primitive sounds coming from outside the open, screened windows, they were in the middle of nowhere.

"Where have you two morons taken me?"

"You're in an old fishing cabin in the Everglades about a hundred miles from—"

Barry punched Larry in the stomach. "Shut up, dummy. She isn't supposed to know where she is. We shouldn't even have been here when she woke up."

"Really," April said, rubbing her sore wrists. "Where *should* you be by now?"

"On our way back home," Larry answered. "But the truck is currently decomissionized."

"Decomissionized? Where did *you* go to school?"

"Harvard," he said proudly.

"You went to Harvard?" April asked incredulously. *"The* Harvard?"

"Nope," Barry said. "He went to the Harvard Young School for Boys in Washington, D.C."

"Yeah, but I love seeing the look on people's faces when I tell them that."

For the first time since she'd been kidnapped, April was able to really get a good look at Barry and Larry. "You guys are just kids. How old are you?"

"Twenty-one," they said in unison.

They didn't look a day over eighteen. They both had smooth, round, baby faces with dark, childlike eyes. If they were slick and cunning as their brother, they would have the perfect naive expressions for drawing in con victims. But fortunately their bulbs were as dim as flashlights with no batteries.

"So you're truck's dead, huh? Then what's the plan? How are you two going to get out of here?"

"Well, Larry thinks he can fix the truck." Barry continued to explain exactly what he felt was wrong with it, causing April's eyes to glaze over. "Then, once he's done working on it, we're outta here. Sorry you can't come with us."

April nodded slowly. "I see. That makes sense. I'm sure it will take a few days for me to starve to death, and maybe a few more weeks for my reeking, decaying corpse to be discovered. By the time they scrape your DNA from beneath my rotting fingernails and determine that the two of you murdered me, you will have had plenty of time to flee the country."

She felt almost cruel watching their stunned little faces go pale.

"You won't starve to death," Barry said, quickly.

"Yeah," Larry agreed. "Before we go, we'll make sure that you have plenty of food to last until your body . . . uh, *you* are discovered."

"We can even make an anonymous call from town letting them know where to find you. I'm sure JB won't mind."

"Well, you boys are just the sweetest. I'm so lucky to have been kidnapped by two guys as thoughtful as you are."

Larry thanked her, and Barry blushed.

"So, once the truck is fixed, you'll bring back a few scraps for me to eat? Because I am a bit hungry now."

Barry stood up and grabbed the bag of corn chips from the table beside his chair. "Here, try these. Larry, get to work on that truck."

"Thanks so much." April buried her hand in the bag and hungrily shoved a handful into her mouth. "But I wish you had tortilla chips. Those are my favorite."

Barry actually got out a pad and wrote it down. "Tortilla chips. Got it."

April leaned back against the pillows, hugging the bag of chips to her chest. This was going to be even easier than she'd thought.

Wednesday nights were Ladies' Night at Blue Paradise, April's favorite night of the week for clubbing. Toni walked up to the entrance and waited in a long line of attractive women who were waiting to get in.

She hadn't been there more than half a second before a husky bouncer walked over and pulled her aside. "What are you doing way back here? Do you want to see me fired? If it gets back to Blue that I let you stand in line, my head would be on the chopping block.''

"Hi, Rutherford. I'm sorry. I certainly don't want to get you into trouble, but I always feel silly stepping in front of all the people who have been waiting before me." She didn't mention that, with the way things were between her and Blue at the moment, she wasn't sure if she still rated her VIP status.

"No problem," he said, placing her hand on his muscular arm. "I'll escort you in."

"Any chance you've seen April tonight?" Her voice was hopeful.

"Sorry, I haven't seen her yet, but I've only been working the door for the last twenty minutes."

"Okay," she said as he guided her into the building. "If you see her, will you let her know I'm looking for her?"

"Sure thing, Toni. Have a good time tonight."

She sighed heavily as he left her. It wasn't likely. She looked around the club. It was still early, and a week night at that. Patrons were clustered at tables, talking in intimate groups as a live jazz band played music. The dance floor was empty.

This had been a waste of time.

"There you are."

Toni looked up and saw Marcus rushing toward her.

"Where's April?" they said in unison.

He stopped in front of her, and they gaped at each other. "She stood me up last night," he said. "I've been calling your house all day."

"The answering machine is broken. I came in late last night—I just assumed April was with you. This afternoon when Natalie called to tell me that April didn't show up for work, I still thought she was with you. I called your home number, and it was busy."

"I was calling around looking for April. I had to go to the center for a while, but I've been running around ever since. When was the last time you saw her?"

Toni clutched her hand to her chest. "Yesterday afternoon. This means she's been missing for at least twenty-four hours. Have you checked the hospitals?"

Toni felt herself swaying on her feet. Something terrible might have happened to her sister, and it might be all her fault. The men who had been following her might have found her sister instead. . . .

Marcus reached out to steady her. "Slow down. Don't start thinking the worst. We can check on the local hospitals and talk to the police. I deal with runaways all the time. We'll go about this methodically. First, let's go back to your house and make sure she hasn't decided to come back on her own."

"Marcus," Toni whispered, feeling as if she were on the edge of hysteria. "We know April did *not* run away from home. She's a twenty-four-year-old woman. If she's missing, it has to be because someone . . ." Toni couldn't even complete the sentence. "You're right. Let's just go back to my house and decide what to do next."

Blue knew he was breaking speed limits as he rounded the corner and entered Toni's condo complex, but he just couldn't shake the terrible feeling growing in the pit of his stomach.

He'd called her house several times, and there wasn't any answer. At Coffee.com they told him that she'd left hours ago. Finally, he'd called Blue Paradise and had hit pay dirt.

Rutherford had seen Toni briefly at the club. He said

she'd left only minutes before Blue called, and that she seemed quite upset about something.

That was all Blue had needed to hear. He parked the car, flew up the walkway to her house, and knocked on the door. When Toni opened it a minute later Blue could see that she looked deflated. Her eyes were dark and heavy, and her skin was pale.

"Blue!" As soon as the name left her left her lips she rushed into his arms. "I'm so glad to see you."

He walked into the house and saw Marcus slumped on the couch. Marcus lifted his hand in greeting.

"What's going on?" Blue asked.

Toni untangled herself from him and stepped back. "April is missing. She never showed up for her date with Marcus, and she didn't come home last night. This morning she didn't go to work at the café."

Marcus nodded. "We were just about to go down to the police station and file a report."

Blue pulled Toni into his arms. "Oh honey, I'm so sorry. Are you okay?"

"Yes. But it's killing me not knowing what happened to April. Will you come to the police station with us?"

"Of course. I'll help in any way that I can."

"Wait a minute," Toni said, looking up at him. "I thought you were supposed to be out of town for a few days. When did you get back?"

"I came straight over from the airport. I got worried when no one answered your phone. Rutherford told me that he'd spoken to you."

"Yes. Our answering machine's broken. I found it on the floor when I came home last night. I thought maybe April dropped it, but for all I know it may have gotten broken in a struggle." Her face began to crumple.

He gave her a reassuring squeeze. "Don't get ahead of yourself. I came home because I was worried about you. I couldn't shake the feeling that something was wrong. That you needed me."

Her eyes widened. "You came home because of me?"

He nodded.

"But what about your friends?"

"I got them started on the right track and headed back here. They understood that I had other priorities."

Blue saw Toni's eyes begin to tear up, so he gave her another little hug. He had to keep her moving. If she stayed busy, she wouldn't have time to dwell on all of the horrible possibilities.

He set her away from him and went into action. "If we're going down to the police station, we want to make sure that they take this missing persons report seriously. Make it clear that she disappeared under suspicious circumstances. They already have a record of most of the incidents regarding you, Toni. That might help."

Marcus stood up. "Let's go."

"Wait, let's get a few things together first to save time. Toni, get the most recent photograph of April that you have. Marcus, why don't you make a list of the names of people she spends time with, and all the places she goes? They're going to ask for that."

Toni didn't question him. She immediately went in search of a photograph. When Marcus finished his list he handed it to Toni to see if she had anything to add.

"Okay, who was the last to see her?"

"I guess I was," Toni said.

"Good. Write down what she was wearing, so you can give the police an accurate description."

"I think she was wearing black rayon shorts and a white blouse."

"Good. Did she take her car?"

"No, it's in the parking lot outside," Marcus said.

"I didn't think anything of it when I came home last

night. I thought Marcus had picked her up. It wasn't until we got back here a few minutes ago that I found her purse lying on the couch. She wouldn't go anywhere without it.''

Marcus looked over at Blue. "You're a quick thinker. I'm familiar with some of the procedure because I talk to the parents of runaways at the center all the time. But I was so upset about April I couldn't think straight. Where did you pick up all this stuff, man?"

"I've had a lot of . . . odd jobs. You'd be surprised what comes to mind when you really need it."

Blue caught Toni watching him. She didn't say anything, but he knew she couldn't help but have suspicions. There wasn't time now, but he'd have a long talk with her and put her mind at ease the first chance he got.

CHAPTER TWELVE

JB paced in his jail cell. Restless energy threatened to overtake him. Now more than ever he needed to get out. Those idiots were going to ruin everything.

His breathing grew heavier as he struggled to control his anger. How was it possible to kidnap a woman by *accident*?

He was in trouble now. Real trouble. He could only hope that they would follow his instructions to the letter this time.

Still, he knew he couldn't count on it. Those two numbskulls hadn't followed a single direction since he'd involved them in this scheme. He had no one to blame but himself. What should have been a simple task had evolved into a full-blown catastrophe.

There was still hope of salvaging this mess if they'd found their way to the cabin he'd sent them to. It was deep in the swamps of the Florida Everglades. All they had to do was take the girl there and leave her. JB would make sure his brothers were long gone by the time the girl was discovered or found her way out on her own.

He hadn't wanted to include them in his disappearing act, but now he had no choice. It was time for Plan B. He hadn't wanted to make bail until he knew his money was waiting for him, and his getaway out of the country had been secured. Now he'd just have to wing it.

The first order of business was making bail so he could retrieve his money himself. It was time to call dear Aunt Eugenia.

After they filed a missing persons' report at the police station, Marcus went home and Blue suggested that Toni spend the night at his place. She hadn't been ready for the apathetic response the police had given her. Blue knew that if they hadn't come so well-prepared, it would have been worse.

To his relief, Toni agreed to stay at his place without protest. Clearly she didn't want to be alone in the house she'd shared with her sister.

Toni came out of the bathroom wearing the T-shirt and shorts she planned to sleep in. Her eyes were red, and she looked exhausted. Blue pulled the cover back on the opposite side of the bed for her to climb in beside him.

She curled next to him and looked up into his eyes. "Thanks for coming back, Blue. I don't know what I would have done without you. I've been wanting to tell you—"

"Shhh. Go to sleep now. We can talk about all that later. Tomorrow we have a big day ahead of us."

Blue knew they hadn't sorted out things between them yet, but he also knew that now wasn't the right time. Toni needed to be comforted, and he wanted to give her whatever she needed.

The next morning Blue made sure he got up before Toni awakened. He had a big day planned. Sitting patiently and waiting for answers would be the worst part of this for Toni. He knew keeping her busy and making her feel useful would help.

He'd just put two bowls of fresh fruit and a tall stack of pancakes on the dining room table when Toni came out of the bedroom. She looked at his preparations and walked over to the table, smiling for the first time since he'd been back.

"You even found a rosebud for the table. It's beautiful. Thank you," she said, touching the small vase in the center of the table.

"It's all for you. You're worth it." He walked over and pulled out her chair.

She looked up at him with a worried expression. "I'm sorry, but I don't think I have much of an appetite."

Blue sat down beside her, shaking his head. "I'm afraid you don't have much of a choice. We have a lot to do today, and I don't want you fainting on me."

"A lot to do? I think I'd better stay home by the—"

Blue picked up her plate, placed three pancakes in the center, and buttered the stack for her. "No. There will be no sitting home by the phone. The first order of business will be to stop by Coffee.com."

She took the plate he offered her and poured the maple syrup he'd warmed for her over them. Half-heartedly, she picked up her knife and fork. "I don't think I'll work today. Maybe tomorrow. If the police are going to find anything out it will probably be today, while the trail is still hot. I don't want to miss—"

"That's why we gave them the number of your cellular phone. You won't miss any calls. I knew you probably wouldn't feel up to working, so I called a couple people from my staff. They're well-trained in restaurant management. They're willing to help out for as long as you need them.''

"But, don't you need them at Blue Paradise?"

"First of all, Blue Paradise doesn't really get busy until after Coffee.com closes. Plus, the place practically runs itself. All I need is for you to go down to the shop and let my staff know what needs to be done. Then you can leave.''

Toni absently lifted a forkful of pancakes to her mouth. "I really appreciate that, Blue. Again, thanks.''

"Okay, enough thank yous, because after we leave your café we've got work to do.''

Nibbling on an orange slice, Toni wrinkled her nose. "What kind of work?''

"We need to talk to your neighbors. Now it's more important than ever that we find out what they may know. I don't think we're going to get much help from the police at this point.''

Toni nodded. "Okay. That sounds good.''

A few minutes later, Blue looked at Toni's plate and laughed. "Well, I'm really sorry that you didn't have an appetite.''

Toni looked down at her empty plate with surprise. "Hey, you tricked me.''

Blue grinned. "It's one of my many talents. No woman will go hungry in my presence.''

Toni was surprised at how quickly the day passed. By the time they got down to Coffee.com there was a lot of work to be done. She realized that she didn't want April to come back and find that she had run their shop into the ground.

Blue's staff arrived around noon. Toni spent a few hours training them on the ins and outs of her business, knowing that if she couldn't come in to work for a few days, everything would keep running like clockwork.

Blue stayed in the background while she did what needed to be done, but it was a tremendous help just knowing that he was there.

Toward the end of the day he walked over to where she stood behind the counter. "I think I have an idea."

"What is it?"

"Well, while you were getting everything settled, I was surfing the net. There are a lot of pages out there dedicated to missing persons. April hasn't been gone that long. Maybe if you set up a page for her, someone who has seen her will contact you."

"That's a great idea. I could probably even make a banner and get a web ring started."

"Banner? Web ring? What are you talking about?"

"I'm sorry. I think making a page for April is perfect. But I was also thinking that if I created a banner with April's picture and a message with a phone number, I might be able to get a few of the more popular sites to put it on their pages."

"How do you get them to do that?"

"Coffee.com sponsors a lot of links to popular sites. I'm hoping that if I contact their web masters, I can convince them to reciprocate by putting April's banner on their sites."

"That's fantastic. I'm sure they'd do it because it's for a good cause."

"Exactly."

With another task at hand, Toni got straight to work. She spent the rest of the afternoon designing a Web page for April and contacting Web sites to post her banner.

After they left Coffee.com that evening, Blue drove her back to her condominium. She made them a couple of sandwiches for dinner, and then they went to talk to her neighbors.

"Do you know which buildings they live in?" Blue asked as they were leaving her house.

"No, but I've seen where they park their cars. Even if they've put them in the shop by now, the reserved spaces have house numbers on them."

"Okay, then that's a good place to start."

They walked around to the other side of Toni's complex. "See over there? I think that blue Toyota Celica belongs to the woman who jumped the curb to avoid hitting us. It looks as if there's a rental car in the space where the man's old gray Chevy used to be. He's the one who actually hit the truck."

"Okay, then let's start with this guy. The space says he lives in two eight oh two."

They approached the house and knocked on the door. After a few minutes a balding, thickset man answered, looking uninviting. "Yes," he said curtly.

Toni started to open her mouth but felt the words lodged in her throat. Blue took over. "We're sorry to bother you, sir. This woman witnessed an accident that occurred in this complex around nine o'clock Friday evening. Do you know anything about that?"

The man's heavy jowled face wrinkled in anger. "Hell, yes, I know all about it." His deepset eyes turned toward Toni. "You were there?"

She nodded slowly.

"Then you saw it. Some idiot comes running into the street, and it's all I can do to keep from hitting him. When I manage to stop just in time, this truck comes flying out of nowhere and slams into me." He clapped his hands together to demonstrate the impact. "Two thousand dollars damage to my front end. That's more than the damn car is worth.''

He turned back to Toni, looking flushed. ''How come I didn't see you there?''

''We're trying to put some pieces of this puzzle together ourselves. When Ms. Rivers came home from work that night the two men who caused the accident began to pursue her, we presume to mug her. She ran, the men followed, and as a result they caused this collision.''

The man nodded, narrowing his eyes. ''Ahh, so you're the one. Well, what do you want from me? Sounds like you know more about the situation than I do.''

''I was wondering if any arrangements were made for the repair of your car. I noticed that you have a rental car outside. Did they exchange insurance information with you, by any chance?''

''Hell, yes. I threatened to call the cops, and they became very cooperative.''

''Ms. Rivers has filed a police report of her own. Having the information that those two men gave you would be very helpful.''

The man eyed them skeptically for a minute, and Toni began to think that he wasn't going to share what he knew.

Finally he shrugged. ''Hold on,'' he said, and shut the door in their faces.

''It's so nice to have such friendly neighbors,'' Toni said under her breath to Blue.

''He doesn't have to be friendly. He just has to tell us what he knows.''

The man reappeared at the door a minute later. He shoved a scrap of paper at them. ''Here. Copy that down.''

Immediately Blue and Toni began searching their

pockets for a pen and paper. Toni looked up to ask the man if he had a sheet of paper for them, but the look on his face deterred her. Blue managed to come up with a pen, and Toni wrote down the information onto an old receipt she had wadded up in her purse.

Toni handed the paper back to the man. "Thanks for your help."

"Yeah," he grunted, and the door slammed shut.

"Okay, that was fun," Toni said sarcastically.

"Let's stop by the woman's house, too."

"What for? We already have the names." She looked down at the scrap of paper. "Barry and Larry Bittle. The rest of the information belongs to the insurance company. It looks like the address for the main corporation in Boston, not their local branch. They could be from anywhere."

"Do the names ring any bells?"

"Not off the top of my head."

"We might as well find out if this woman has anything to add."

They rang the doorbell of the condo corresponding with the sporty Toyota's space number. Toni recognized the woman from the scene of the accident immediately. She was wearing shorts that would have fit a Barbie doll more comfortably, and a neon tank top that was helpless to conceal the black bra she wore beneath.

She took one look at Blue and opened the door wide. "Hi! What can I do for you?"

Blue repeated what he'd told the man and she instantly invited them in. The best way to describe her place was "over-decorated". Knickknacks and thinga-mabobs covered every surface, and the brightly colored furniture was covered with cat hair.

"My name's Cassandra." She grabbed Blue's arm and dragged him over to a chair. "Can I get you anything?"

Blue introduced Toni and then himself. "No thanks. We just wanted to ask a few questions about the accident, and then we'll be on our way."

Toni, not wanting to get cat hair stuck to her black shorts, chose to stand beside Blue's chair. She was beginning to get annoyed with all the attention Cassandra was showing him, so she decided to take charge.

"So Cassandra, do you remember the two men who were driving the red truck?"

"Oh yes, they were very nice." She looked toward Blue to clarify. "I got a little bit upset over the whole thing. I can be such a crybaby. After all, I'd come *this* close to running someone over."

Cassandra looked up at Toni with censure in her eyes. "It was *you*, wasn't it? Don't you know it's dangerous to roller-skate in the middle of the street like that?"

"I wasn't roller skating," Toni said, feeling her temper rise. "I was trying to escape those two criminals that you thought were so nice."

Blue put a hand on Toni's arm, letting her know that he would take it from there. He explained that the two men were chasing Toni through the parking lot, and asked Cassandra if she remembered anything else the men may have said.

"I don't know. As I said, I was very upset. Everyone was so helpful in trying to calm me down."

"I'll just bet they were," Toni whispered.

Blue gave her a warning look.

"Did they give you their names and insurance information?" he asked.

"No. My car wasn't damaged. I was just shaken up when I had to jump the curb. Wait, they did tell me that they were from out of town."

"Did they say where?" Blue asked.

"I think they said Columbia."

"The city or the country?" Toni asked warily. She didn't trust this woman's memory.

The woman clapped her hand to her forehead. "Wait. I think it was the *District* of Columbia."

"Washington, D.C. Thank you, that helps a lot," Blue said, standing up. "If you think of anything else, will you give us a call?"

The woman walked them to the door, giving Blue a long look. "Sure. I'd be happy to call you."

As they walked back to her home, Toni was quiet.

"What's wrong?" Blue asked.

Toni stopped dead in her tracks. "I think I just figured out who those two men are."

April was sitting up, watching The Home Shopping Network on the shack's tiny, cable-ready TV when Barry and Larry finally came inside. They'd been spending all their time working on the truck. While they were doing that, April had been working on a two-part plan. It was time for stage one.

"The truck is finally working. We're going to have to be leaving soon," Barry said.

April gave them a doe-eyed look. "Would you mind picking up a few things at the store for me before you go? I made just a teensy-weensy little list." She handed it to Larry.

Larry took the scrap of paper, then jumped as a high-pitched, shrill noise came from his waist. The two brothers instantly started swearing. Larry pulled the offending cellular phone from his belt and threw it to Barry. "You talk to him."

"Oh no. I explained about April. It's your turn." Barry caught it as if it were a hot potato and threw it back.

April stood up and caught the phone when it came sailing in Barry's direction. "I'll talk to him. I have a few words for our friend the jailbird."

She hit the answer button. "Hello."

"Who the hell is this?"

"Well, who the hell is *this?*"

"I must have dialed the wrong number," he muttered to himself.

"No, JB, a.k.a. Jordan Banks. You've got the right number, and I've got *your* number. This is April Rivers."

JB cursed violently.

She clucked her tongue. "My my. I thought jail was supposed to be rehabilitating. Seems to me you're just picking up more bad habits."

"Where are my brothers?"

"They're right here. They were fighting over who would have the privilege of talking to you, so I claimed the honor for myself."

"Fine, April, let's talk. My brothers tell me that you and your sister came into a lot of money recently. You started some computer coffee bar. Where'd you get the money for a venture like that?"

"Oh JB, it's so sweet of you to show an interest in our good fortune. We won the lottery. If you're hoping to get in on the action, you ought to know that all of the money is tied up in our new business."

"You won the lottery, huh? Is that where your sister told you it came from?"

"She didn't have to tell me. I bought her the ticket myself. Where else could she have gotten that kind of money from?"

"Never mind. Put my brothers on the phone."

"One more thing—what exactly did you send your brothers out here to do? Let me guess. Did you hide a cache of treasure in the false bottom of my sister's wardrobe, or what? What exactly are you after?''

"Put my brother's on the phone. Now!''

"It was nice talking to you, too.'' April sighed, and instead of handing over the phone she clicked the OFF button.

The two brothers stood staring at her, looking worried. "What did he say?''

"Oh, he just sends his love.'' April quickly gestured toward her shopping list. "The sooner you two run along to the store, the sooner you can get on your way.''

They exchanged looks, nodded, and headed out to the truck.

April held her breath as she listened to the engine start. Luckily, they hadn't noticed that they'd left her with their phone.

CHAPTER THIRTEEN

"I can't believe my ex-boyfriend, Jordan Banks—or James Bittle, or whatever his name is—has something to do with this," Toni said, sitting next to Blue at the kitchen table. Ever since they'd gotten back to the house she'd been trying to make some sense of the situation.

Blue took a sip of the chocolate almond coffee she'd just poured for him. "Well, from what you've told me, it's the only explanation that makes sense. He's a known con artist, and he was arrested unexpectedly. It seems obvious that he left something valuable in your care—without your knowledge, of course—and now he's sent his brothers to retrieve it."

"Okay. Well, clearly, I don't have it anymore, or they would have found it the first time they broke in." Toni smoothed her hair back from her face in frustration. "What I can't figure out is why they would take April."

"She probably surprised them while they were searching your place the second time around."

"So they took her with them? What does that mean? They wanted to shut her up for good because she can identify them? If that's true, then I may never—"

Blue reached across the table to pick up Toni's hand. He gave it a comforting squeeze. "I don't think so. Your ex-boyfriend went to jail for running cons. Not murder. It makes more sense that they plan to trade the money, drugs, or whatever for April."

"Then shouldn't we have heard from them by now?"

"There are no hard and fast rules about this. We know you have something they want. That's why they kept showing up over these past few weeks. My guess is that they aren't too bright—otherwise they wouldn't have given your neighbors their real names."

"Great. This is just getting better. My sister was kidnapped by a couple of stupid criminals. How come that's not reassuring?"

"Look, Toni, I've seen these situations before. At this stage of the game, no news is good news. If they're as inexperienced as I think they are, they're probably still sorting their way through this. For all we know, they may be waiting to flee the area before they let us know where she is. I honestly don't believe that they've hurt her in any way."

Toni didn't bother asking how he'd seen this type of situation before, or why he was so certain that April was okay. All she knew was that he wouldn't lie to her. When he told her it was going to be all right, she believed him.

"I can't believe Jordan is still haunting me after all this time." She stood up from the table. "I wonder what it is he's hidden. Do you think it may still be here?"

Blue shrugged. "My guess is that when he sent his brothers here he told them exactly where to find whatever it is he wants. They obviously didn't. Did you get rid of anything before you moved?"

Toni threw up her hands. "You name it. I gave boxes and boxes of stuff to The Salvation Army."

"Any furniture?"

"Maybe an end table or two. A couple of lamps. Odds and ends I had left over from college—a mini-refrigerator and a futon. Stuff like that."

"He could have easily hidden something in any one of those things. Most likely your boy's just out of luck. Sounds like you've already gotten rid of his valuable merchandise."

"Maybe I should go back to D.C. and pay him a visit. If I let him know that I don't have whatever it is he's looking for, maybe he can tell his brothers to back off."

"Don't get ahead of yourself—"

The ringing of the telephone interrupted Toni's sentence. It was her cellular phone. "Oh my gosh. That has to be news about April."

She flew across the room to answer it. "Hello?"

"Hey, Sis. What's up?"

"April? Oh my God. Are you all right? Where are you?"

"Slow down. I'm okay. You'll never believe what happened."

"Let me guess. You came home while Jordan Bank's idiot twin brothers were searching the house for some mysterious cache, and they took you with them."

"Wow. You're good. Anyway, I suckered them out of their cell phone and sent them off to the store, but they may realize it's gone and come back any minute. I didn't want you to think that I was dead. I know how dramatic you can be."

Toni clutched the phone. It was a relief to hear her

sister's voice, but she couldn't believe how casual April was acting. "Can you tell me where you are?"

Blue handed Toni a pad and paper. "Write down what she's saying," he whispered.

"All I know is that I'm in a rundown little fishing cabin somewhere in the Everglades. I'm a hundred miles from something, but I don't know what."

Toni continued jotting notes as she talked. "What do you see when you look out the windows?"

"Nothing. It's pretty dark now, but even during the day all I can see are a bunch of ugly old trees and tall grass for miles. They've got me in the middle of nowhere."

"Don't worry, April. We'll find you. The important thing is that you're all right. They didn't hurt you, did they?"

"No, actually they've been pretty cool. Thank goodness they have a cable-ready TV out here. At least I can watch The Home Shopping Network."

"You've been watching television. Are you kidding me?"

"Nope. They must have wrecked the truck on the way out here. They spent most of the day fixing it. I think they plan to leave me here. But they promised to let someone know where to find me once they've gotten far enough away."

"They're going to leave you there?" Toni felt a lump rising in her throat.

Blue was reading her notes from over her shoulder. He reached out and took the phone from her.

"April, this is Blue. We're going to find you, okay? I just need you to do one thing for me. Keep them there. Pretend you're sick. Whatever you have to do. Just don't let them leave. Do you think you can do that? Great."

He handed the phone back to Toni. She told her

sister that she loved her, and then they said their good-byes. Toni exhaled a long breath as she turned off the phone. "That was it. She's gone."

Blue guided her over to the couch. "Okay, she didn't give us much to work with, but I think we can find her."

"How? She barely told us anything. The police have been so uncooperative that I doubt they'd bother taking the time to help us get to her."

"That's why we're going to have to take care of this on our own."

Toni shook her head. "I still don't see how."

Blue got up and walked over to her phone. "I spend a lot of time doing favors for friends. I think I might know a few people who can help us."

April was curled up in a beat-up recliner when the brothers returned. The phone was across the room on a table, where she was ignoring it as though it had been there all along.

Larry came in and handed April a bag. "Um, you didn't tell me what kind, so I got the ultra thin with wings. Is that okay?"

She looked in the bag, resisting the urge to giggle. "Those will do, but you got the wrong shade of nail polish. I asked for Spicy Peach. This is Juicy Apricot."

Barry came inside behind him. "I told you. I told you that wasn't the right one."

April took some cotton balls out of the bag and uncapped the nail polish remover. "That's okay. This will do for now. Did you remember to get my tortilla chips?"

Barry proudly held up a jumbo-size bag of chips. April smiled and nodded toward the rickety, three-legged table beside the lumpy, easy chair she was sitting in. "Just put them over there."

"Sure thing," Barry said, eager to please as he threw Larry a smug grin.

April clutched her stomach. "I'll eat them when I'm feeling better."

Larry knelt down beside her. "What's wrong? Are you okay?"

She doubled over, groaning in mock pain. "I'm not feeling too well." She reached out and grabbed Larry's shirt. "Promise me you won't leave me like this. I hate to be alone when I'm sick."

Once again the brothers exchanged looks. "Of course we wouldn't leave you."

April smiled off to the side, where they couldn't see her expression. She had these two wrapped around her little finger.

CHAPTER FOURTEEN

Toni's body vibrated tension as she paced her living room floor. There was nothing worse than waiting. Her ears were so finely tuned to the phone, listening for its ring, that her heart nearly leapt out of her chest when it finally did.

It was Blue, and he was all business. "Okay, this is what I want you to do. Pack light—one change of clothes. Dress in jeans and a long-sleeved shirt, multiple layers. Wear the heaviest shoes you have. Hiking boots would be ideal. If you don't have those, whatever winter boots you wore back in D.C. should be fine."

Toni bit her lip. "I think I gave most of my winter accessories to the Salvation Army."

"We're going into a large primitive area. Swamp land. Likely, there will be snakes and other less than charming creatures. You'll need something thick, with treads."

"I think April has a pair of combat boots she used

to wear when they were the latest fashion rage. She and I are the same shoe size.''

''Perfect. Collect your things quickly and meet me in my office at Blue Paradise. I've given Marcus the same instructions.''

Toni hung up the phone and rushed to get ready. She didn't want to be the weak link in this chain. She had to keep up with two rugged men who had their masculine hormones on overdrive to rescue a damsel in distress. More than anything she was grateful that Blue hadn't tried to convince her to wait at home because the two of them would be able to move faster without her.

Throughout this ordeal he'd kept her from losing her mind. He'd kept her busy, knowing that feeling useful was the best thing to fight the panic that rose in her chest every time she thought about her sister.

Toni had no idea what kind of ''odd jobs'' Blue had done in his past—and she didn't need to know. The point was that she was grateful for it. Without whatever special training and connections he'd managed to build, she'd still be waiting for the police to get around to helping her sister.

When Toni entered Blue's office with a canvas backpack slung over her shoulder, Marcus was already there. Blue wore jeans and a hooded sweatshirt, with a wilderness vest covered in pockets. He sat on the sofa, packing up a first aid kit.

''Hi, Toni.'' Marcus was sitting beside him with a look of pure awe on his face. ''Have you seen this guy's stash? Whoo!''

Toni had a feeling it wasn't Blue's first aid kit that Marcus was impressed with.

Blue looked up. ''We're just about ready to go.'' He

crossed toward her, looking over her outfit approvingly.
"Perfect."

He leaned down and kissed her lightly, taking a
moment to give her a gentle squeeze. "Are you all set?"

She held up her backpack. "Upon inspection, I'm
sure you'll find that it holds up to the Blue Cooper
regulations, sir."

"Great." He walked back over and checked through
his supplies. Clearly he was ticking off a mental list. "I
just need one more thing."

He walked back toward what Toni had always thought
was an empty closet. He came out with some kind of
handgun and a box of cartridges. Walking back to the
table, he began loading the gun.

Toni was speechless.

Blue spoke without looking up. "To answer all your
unspoken questions . . . no, I don't expect to need this,
but it's important to have it, just in case. Yes, it's legal,
and I have a license to carry it."

Toni opened her mouth to speak, thinking he was
finished. He wasn't.

"No, I don't keep a cache of weapons in my coat
closet because running a nightclub in West Palm Beach
is such a dangerous business. I keep them there because
I know they're safe and, since I don't need them as
often as I used to, they've become more of a collection
than anything else."

The gun loaded, Blue looked up to meet her eyes.
"Okay?"

All Toni could do was nod vigorously in response.
She locked gazes with Marcus. He gave her the thumbs
up, looking as hyped as a professional wrestler promot-
ing his next tag team match.

* * *

The three of them piled into Blue's sport utility vehicle and started south on Florida's turnpike. The Everglades were about two-and-a-half hours from West Palm Beach.

They were able to stick to main highways for most of the drive, but once they got into the Everglades the roads became more rural. The farther they drove, the rougher it got. Blue didn't talk much for most of the trip, but Marcus seemed as if he'd been pumped full of adrenaline. He couldn't stop talking.

Toni absorbed most of Marcus's nervous energy. For her part, they couldn't get there quick enough. She was about ready to jump out of her skin, and it was all she could do to not keep asking if they were almost there. Keeping up her end of the conversation with Marcus could only distract her so much.

"I can't wait to see April." Marcus's voice came from the backseat. "I know we haven't been together long, but I've never met anyone like her. She's funny and out there sometimes, but she's also down to earth . . . and real. It usually takes me years to feel I really know someone, but I felt that way with her after only a week."

"Yeah." Toni's answer implied that she understood, but she really didn't. She'd known Blue for roughly the same amount of time as Marcus and April had known each other. It was true that she felt closer to him than she had to anyone else she'd dated. But somehow she didn't think that was what Marcus was talking about.

"Sounds as if you and April are pretty serious."

"Yes. If I hadn't been sure before—which I was—being apart from her now proves it." The pang in his voice was evident.

Toni looked over at Blue's profile. He hadn't said a

word during this entire conversation. His mind was fixed on driving and reading the compass on the dashboard. Every so often he'd ask her to show him the hand-drawn map his friend had faxed them.

How would she feel if Blue disappeared? As if someone had ripped out her heart.

Before she could think about that any further Blue let out an angry curse, and the truck came rumbling to a halt.

"What's wrong?" she and Marcus asked at the same time.

Blue cut off the engine. "I think we have a flat."

They all climbed out of the truck. Toni stood back while Blue and Marcus examined the damage. She looked around. The terrain had looked uncultivated from inside the vehicle, but up close it was downright savage.

The air was thick and humid. Though she had her hair tied back from her face, Toni could feel it beginning to droop, soaking up the air like a sponge. Gnarled, bent trees overgrown with vines and moss hovered over them, closing them in. The grass grew wild and untamed all around them, hiding whatever crawled on the muddy, sodden earth.

Toni began lifting her feet, remembering Blue's warning about snakes and other less than charming creatures. Suddenly she was certain something would reach out and grab her ankle at any moment. She was tempted to go sit in the truck, but she didn't want to appear to be the fragile female while the men did all the work.

Blue turned to her, dusting his hands off on his jeans. "We have a problem."

"What's wrong? Don't you have a spare?"

Marcus stood up behind Blue. "Oh, we've got a spare,

but the axle on the wheel is bent. Even if we could change the tire, the truck wouldn't drive straight."

She felt her jaw go slack. "Are you kidding me? How could this happen? I thought these trucks were built for rough terrain like this."

Blue sighed heavily. "I think we must have rolled over a huge rock a few miles back. It threw the truck out of alignment."

Toni moved closer to Blue, still worried about what might be lurking at her feet. Evening was approaching fast. "So what do we do now?"

Blue got the map out of the truck. "Actually we're very close to where my buddy says the cabin should be. We could probably hike the rest of the way."

"Hike?" Toni was on the verge of hysteria. "We barely had a road to drive on, and you want to hike? If your huge macho truck couldn't handle the trek, what makes you think we can?"

"You'd rather wait here, when we could be at the cabin in less than an hour?" Blue asked. He looked to Marcus for reinforcement.

Marcus backed up against the truck and folded his arms. "I'm staying out of this. Whatever you all decide is cool with me."

"What are we going to do when we get there? We won't even have a vehicle to drive April home in."

Blue reached into the truck and handed Toni her backpack and a flashlight. "We'll radio the police from here and tell them to meet us at the cabin. Come on, we're wasting time."

Sighing in resignation, Toni secured the bag to her back. There was little point in arguing. Blue had gotten them this far. If he felt they could hike the rest of the way, then they would hike.

"If I get fatally bitten by anything, tell April that she

can have the purple suede suit she's been after, but I want to be buried in my Ferragamo shoes.''

Toni had never been so tired in her life. She trudged behind Blue and in front of Marcus, supposedly for her own safety. Unfortunately that hadn't prevented her from getting up close and personal with mud a few times when an overgrown tree root decided to pop up unexpectedly.

Her legs ached with unrelenting pain, and her skin itched from the mud and the humidity, but Toni refused to complain. Blue and Marcus were marching along as if they were on an evening stroll, and she didn't want them to think she couldn't keep up.

Blue looked over his shoulder, as he did every two yards. "How are you doing? Are you okay? Need to rest?"

She *wanted* to rest. Oh, how she longed to stretch out on a soft bed and just . . . not move for a day or so. But the idea of stopping long enough for the creepy crawlies out there to feast on her was enough to keep her moving despite her screaming muscles.

"I'm okay. Let's just get there." Her mouth was dry and cottony, and she'd give anything for one of Blue's godforsaken Yoo-hoos. Now that she thought about it, she'd bet anything that he had one stashed in that survival pack of his.

Before Toni got carried away enough to climb on his back and attack him for his rations, Blue stopped and pointed in front of them.

"There—up ahead. I think that's it."

Toni saw the tiny shack, and it looked like a sprawling Beverly Hills mansion to her tired brain. Her legs regained enough energy to carry her forward. She could see the light at the end of the tunnel, pumping adrenaline into her veins.

The three of them came up to the shack from the back. Blue turned to her as they crept around to the front door. "Let Marcus and I enter first. I'll call for you when I'm sure everything is safe. Okay?"

"Yes. I got it."

When they reached the entrance, Blue and Marcus burst inside like a couple of commandos. Toni listened, waiting for the cabin to erupt with chaotic noise. Instead she heard dead silence, except for a heartfelt curse from Marcus.

"Toni." Blue called her name softly and she rushed inside, realizing immediately what had caused Marcus to swear so savagely.

April and her two captors had fallen asleep in front of the television set. An old Eddie Murphy movie was playing, and there was a big bowl of popcorn on the floor beside them. Her sister was tucked into an old, worn recliner, sleeping with her head resting on the curve of her arm.

The other two were sprawled on the floor at her feet, out cold.

Toni, Marcus, and Blue just stood there, exchanging dumbfounded looks. That's where the county police found them a minute later.

"Are they dead?" asked the first officer on the scene.

"No," Blue answered, shaking his head incredulously. "They're asleep."

CHAPTER FIFTEEN

"And then the three of them burst into the cabin like the cavalry, coming to rescue me." April stood in front of a laughing audience at Coffee.com.

Toni and April had decided to celebrate April's homecoming with a special event at the Internet café. They created a Web site called Wild Rivers, outlining their recent adventures and inviting everyone to come to Coffee.com to hear them tell the story.

So far the event was a great success. The shop was filled with customers, and everyone had gathered around the center stage. April stood in front of the giant screen Web TV, giving her version of the rescue. Toni, Blue, Marcus, and April had each taken a piece of the story to recount, while the others interjected at will.

"Yes, we thought she needed rescuing," Toni spoke up. "But after driving for hours and then trekking through miles of snake-infested swampland, we finally get to the cabin, prepared to rescue April from her heartless captors, and what do we find?''

"They were asleep," Blue jumped in. "It seems that watching movies and eating popcorn had been too much for them. Apparently they took the *nap* in kidnapping just a little too seriously."

"Right," Marcus added. "While we were home worrying about April's safety she was having a relaxing vacation—painting her toenails, eating junk food, and watching cable TV. Some kidnapping."

"I don't think kidnap is the right word. Let's just call it involuntary relocation." April laughed, walking over to Marcus and stepping into his arms. "And it wasn't as great as you all are making it sound. That rinky-dink little television set only got five channels."

Blue took April's place to wrap things up. "The good news is that the two men who relocated April involuntarily were arrested. We hope you've enjoyed Coffee.com's presentation of Crooks Are Stupid."

The audience laughed and clapped, and Toni was about to thank everyone for coming when Marcus led April back out onto the stage.

She looked up at Blue when he joined her on the sidelines. "What's going on?"

He shrugged. "I don't know. They didn't mention anything to me."

Marcus turned to April and got down on one knee in front of her.

"Oh my God," Toni said, clapping her hand to her mouth. The audience howled and whistled, and then fell silent.

"April, being away from you these past few days has made me realize I don't ever want to be apart from you again. I love you, and I want to spend the rest of my life with you. Will you marry me?"

April's hands flew to her cheeks. "Yes! I can't believe this. Yes, yes, yes."

Marcus slipped a ring onto her finger, despite the nervous shaking of her hand. Then he stood and pulled her into a tight embrace, and the audience gave them a standing ovation.

Toni turned to Blue with tears welling in her eyes. "This is incredible." A combination of emotions was swirling through her. "My sister's getting married."

The four of them went out to dinner to celebrate Marcus and April's good news. Then the newly engaged couple went off together and Blue drove Toni home.

Blue sat on her couch and picked up the weekend section of the newspaper. He looked at his watch. "It's only eight o'clock. Do you want to go to a movie or something?"

Toni knelt on the couch, facing him. She took the paper out of his hands. "Or something." Now that April was home safe and things were back to normal, it was time for them to concentrate on their relationship again. Lately, it was all Toni could think about.

Blue grinned, correctly reading the seductive look in her eyes. "What? You'd rather talk?"

She put two hands on his chest. "No."

He placed his hands over hers. "Ahh, then do you want to play chess? I'm pretty good at board games."

"No, thanks," Toni whispered, leaning forward to press her lips against his.

Blue instantly scooped her up into his arms. "Okay, I can take a hint," he said, carrying her off to the bedroom.

Toni didn't want to rush things, though. She knew it was long past time for her to stop hiding from her feelings. Blue was indeed true. He'd proven that he was loyal and honest, not with words but with his actions. She had to stop judging him by standards set by other men, and start appreciating him for who he was.

And she intended to start with tonight.

Blue set her on her feet in her bedroom and started tugging his shirt out of his pants. Toni placed a hand on his to stop him. "Not so fast."

She motioned toward the bed. "Make yourself comfortable. I'll do the rest."

Blue propped himself up on the bed with his ankles crossed and his fingers interlaced behind his head, while Toni walked around the room lighting candles. Then she took off her clothes and changed into a short silk robe. She wanted to make sure that Blue knew this night was for him.

She came back into the room carrying a bottle of scented massage oil. "Did I tell you that I'm one of only eight other people in the country who know the exotic art of Chinese oil massage?"

His gorgeous blue eyes immediately lit up. "I don't believe you did. Care to demonstrate?"

"It would be my pleasure."

She undressed him slowly, first unbuttoning his shirt and letting her fingers lightly graze his skin. After she dragged the shirt from his large muscular arms, she took off his shoes and socks and then unfastened his pants. She felt his sharp intake of breath as her hands brushed against him. Once his pants were gone, he had only one last barrier to protect him from her hungry eyes.

She stripped him of that scrap of material quickly, revealing his hard, well-muscled, golden body.

"Be gentle with me," he said, closing his eyes and resting his head on the pillows.

Toni poured the oil into her palm and then heated it by vigorously rubbing her hands together. She smoothed the oil all over his body, kneading his muscles with her fingers. Blue moaned as her hands worked on him.

She turned him over and set upon his broad back, steadily working her way down to his firm, round buttocks. There she molded and teased the warm cheeks, continuing down from the backs of his thighs to his knees and calves. She gave the soles of his feet special attention, loving the satisfied murmurings from deep within his throat.

Finally, she turned him onto his back again and started all over with her mouth. She nibbled her way from his neck to his masculine nipples, letting her tongue circle them into peaks.

She continued down, brushing her lips over the flat wall of muscle beneath his ribs, taking the time to dip her tongue into the indentation of his navel.

Blue was hard and ready when she made it to the center of his body. She tasted him, gently first with her tongue. He moaned her name, bucking his hips.

That was all the encouragement Toni needed. She held him firmly in her hands and let her mouth devour him. With her tongue, teeth, and lips, she pleasured him until he was begging her to stop.

"Come here," he whispered. Reaching out, he pulled her up to him until she was straddling his waist. He untied the belt of her robe and parted it so his hands could cover her breasts, causing her nipples to bead like dark pearls.

"You're so beautiful," he said, taking her face in his hands and bringing her lips to meet his in a long kiss.

"I love you," Toni whispered. She reached down to put him into position so she could slide down on him.

They both groaned at the sweet thrill of their bodies connecting.

Swivelling her hips, Toni took control, riding him the way a kayak would ride a wild wave. Blue's body moved with the force and unpredictability of an ocean beneath her. They floated together and drifted apart. She sank down on him and he flowed into her.

Finally, their waves built at once, cresting into beautiful peaks of sensation before their bodies collapsed together in the aftermath of their loving.

Blue sank back into the pillows on Toni's bed, feeling two things—satisfaction and wariness. He was satisfied because he and Toni had an incredible sex life. He was wary because he sensed a heavy conversation was about to follow.

She wasn't sure about him. Sure, during this past week he'd proved that she could count on him, and she was grateful for that. She couldn't thank him enough. But when it came right down to it, he still didn't know if she trusted him. Toni'd had too many disappointments with men for him to have hope.

Toni curled against his back, stroking his arms. "Blue, we need to talk."

Here it comes. He almost said the words out loud. Instead he turned over to face her. "What's on your mind?"

"Us."

He nodded, supporting his head in the palm of his hand. "Okay. I'm listening."

She sat up and faced him, squeezing a pillow to her chest. "We never really had a chance to have that talk about our big argument last week."

Blue sighed. "I've had a lot of time to think about

that too, Toni. I think you were right. I was pushing for more in this relationship than you were ready to give."

She nodded. "I wasn't ready then, but I am now. I'm sorry that I implied that I didn't trust you, Blue, because I really do. And if that offer to move in with you is still open—even though the 'danger' is behind us—then I'd like to take you up on it."

Blue sat up too, shaking his head. "Toni, don't do this."

"Don't do what? Have you changed your mind ... about us?"

"No. I haven't changed my mind, and I don't think you have, either. It's going to take time, and we can't move forward until *both* of us are ready."

"That's what I'm trying to tell you. I'm ready."

Blue had to caution himself not to get eager. She was finally saying the words he'd been waiting to hear, but he knew there was more to it. "Toni, I saw your face today. When Marcus put that ring on April's finger—yes, you were happy, but I know what you were thinking. Part of you couldn't believe your baby sister might get married before you."

Toni was quiet for a minute. Blue was certain it was because the truth of his words was finally sinking it.

"I'm not going to say that part of this doesn't have to do with seeing Marcus and April together, but not for the reasons you think. I've been thinking about us a lot, and I know I've been letting my history with other men cloud our relationship. I've tried holding you at arm's length, when all I've really wanted was to share my life with you."

Blue wanted to believe her, but Toni wasn't the only one with a bad relationship in her past. He had a lot at stake, too.

"Marriage," she said. "Family. Those things have

always been important to me. It's only recently that I've tried to convince myself to focus on those things later. But now I'm seeing that I've been living someone else's rules. I don't know whose, but they weren't my own. The fact is, the things I don't know about you don't matter. I know who you are. I know what kind of person you are. And that's the person I love. That's the person I want to be with.''

Blue took a deep breath. He didn't like what he was about to say, but he knew he had to.

''Are you sure about that?'' He held up a hand to stop her when she tried to answer. ''I know you think you are, but I'm not sure you know what you're getting into.''

He let his words hang in the air before continuing.

''You were right about one thing, Toni. You don't know all there is to know about me. I'm not always cheerful and upbeat. I don't always crack jokes and make wisecracks. That's only one side of me.''

She nodded. ''I've begun to see that.''

''You have no idea,'' he said, shaking his head. ''I can't risk completely letting you in until I know you're ready. You aren't the only one with bad memories, Toni. You aren't the only one who doesn't want to repeat past mistakes.''

Blue stood up and began putting his clothes back on.

Toni leapt to her feet. ''Where are you going?''

''I'm going home. I think we both need some space to think.''

''Wait. Can't we talk about this?''

He grabbed his wallet and his keys. ''We'll talk soon. I just think it's best if I go now.''

Blue left Toni's house, trying not to think about the stricken look on her face.

* * *

Toni lay in bed that night, unable to sleep. All she could think about was the fact that she'd managed to blow it with Blue.

She stared without blinking up at the ceiling, replaying her conversation with him over and over in her head. Then she heard a loud crash in the living room.

When the hall light didn't come on, indicating that April had come home from her date, she sat straight up in bed. She looked over at the clock on her night stand. It was only ten o'clock.

She heard more banging and another crash. With her heart hammering in her chest, Toni reached for the telephone. Then the hall light came on.

"April?" she called.

"No. It isn't April," a male voice called back.

Toni flew out of the bed, looking for a weapon to protect herself with. She grabbed the first thing she laid her hands on—the lamp on her night stand. Yanking the cord out of the wall, she gripped it tightly and swung it high in the air, like a bat.

She almost dropped it on the floor when Jordan Banks appeared in her doorway. "Come on, Antoinette, aren't you happy to see me? I'm *very* happy to see you." His eyes raked over her thin gown.

Exhaling in a long rush, Toni felt more anger than fear. This man had ruined her life in so many ways. If he thought he was just going to waltz into her home and offer up a second helping, he was in for a rude awakening.

She dropped the lamp on the bed and pulled on her long, terry cloth bathrobe. "What the hell are you doing here? Last I knew, they were measuring you for a striped suit."

He shrugged. "Stripes aren't a good look for me. Besides, I'm out on bail."

"Here's a news flash, Jordan—or whatever your real name is—you aren't supposed to cross state lines. When they find out that you have, you'll be behind bars permanently."

He laughed. "You can call me JB."

Toni found it hard to believe she'd ever found his slick, too perfect looks attractive.

"It doesn't matter if they find out I jumped bail. I'm not going back. That's why you and I are going to have a little talk."

"We have nothing to talk about."

He stepped toward her. "I think we do."

Toni wasn't sure what to do next, but she knew she didn't like being cornered in her bedroom. "Fine. We'll talk in the living room. Wait there while I put some clothes on."

He shook his head. "I'm sorry, babe, but I can't let you out of my sight. I never could get enough of looking at you—that curvy little body of yours and all that smooth brown skin—but of course my favorite was always your tight little—"

"Okay," Toni said sharply, just to shut him up. "Then we'll both go out to the living room together."

"After you." He stepped aside so she could pass.

Toni had a lot of trouble keeping her back to him. She kept waiting to feel the blade of a knife stabbing her.

JB made himself comfortable on her sofa. Toni sat on the other side of the room, with a table between them. "How did you get in here?" she asked.

He waved her off. "I thought you read my rap sheet. I learned to pick locks before I learned to read."

"Well, aren't you clever? Now, would you mind telling

me why you decided to pay me, of all people, a visit. I thought it should be clear by now that I don't have whatever it is you sent your brothers down here to get. The fact that they're safe behind bars is a hint that maybe you'd want to steer clear of me."

"Ahh, my lovely Antoinette. You have changed, haven't you?" He looked around the room. "You've made a new life for yourself. Set yourself up in a new business. I hear it's doing pretty well."

"Why don't you make your point?"

"Where did you get the money for all this?"

For some reason that question struck Toni as funny, and she found herself laughing out loud.

"You know Jordan, I mean JB, not everyone is as crooked as you are. My sister bought a winning lottery ticket for my birthday."

It was his turn to laugh. "Isn't that a convenient story? It must have felt like winning the lottery when you found my bearer bonds."

"I don't even know what bearer bonds look like. Why don't you tell me exactly why you think I would have yours?"

"Because I hid them in one of those Men Who Hate to Love Women books you like to read."

Toni's jaw dropped. "Why would you do something like that? It doesn't sound as if you intended them to be a gift."

He ignored her last statement. "I was tipped off that the IRS had started nosing around. I didn't want them to know I had any assets if they decided to audit me, so I had to get them out of my hands for a while. All I had to do was slip them in between the book and the jacket cover of one of your books and glue the edges down. Then I put the book back on your shelf. I had no way of knowing that I'd be picked up on a DWI charge before I could go back for them.''

"Oh, what a shame," Toni said, but the gears of her brain were turning quickly.

If JB had hidden his bonds in one of her books, then she knew without a doubt that she no longer had it. She'd sent all the self-help relationship books to The Salvation Army. Some lucky recipient was going to open one of her books and find a small fortune.

It made her smile to know that he would never see his money again. "Sounds like poetic justice to me. You were incarcerated before you could enjoy the money that you probably swindled some poor sucker out of, anyway."

"Now that's where you're wrong, Antoinette. Those bearer bonds are probably the only money I've ever had that I actually had a right to. My Aunt Eugenia's husband, Uncle Frank, passed away last fall, and decrepit old Aunt Eugenia has always been generous with the funds if you help her out around the house. I was flat broke at the time, and thought I could get her to slip me a couple of hundred if I packed up the old man's junk for her."

While JB talked, Toni was cooking up a little con job of her own.

"Before I left she gave me a few boxes of the old man's stuff to dispose of, plus old trunk that she said I could keep. Don't you know the old geezer had the mother lode in bearer bonds locked up in there? I don't know what he was saving up for—maybe to leave the old battle axe. Hell if I know. All I knew is that they were mine, on top of the five hundred bucks the old lady gave me to get rid of the junk."

"Well, that's a beautiful story, JB, but what are you

going to do when I tell you that I don't have those books anymore?"

He didn't blink an eye, as though he had expected to hear that story. "Spent it already? That's fine. Since you don't have my property, I'll just have to leave here with some of yours. You must have a few bucks left over from your *lottery* winnings. After that, I just help myself to whatever valuables you keep here in the house. But don't think you'll be rid of me even then. I'll be disappearing soon, but I have connections all over. I'll just keep hitting you up and hitting you up until I've gotten my money's worth out of you."

He saw her purse lying on the table beside the sofa. "We'll start with this." He pulled out her wallet and shoved the cash and all her credit cards into his pockets. He stood, looking around. "Let's see what else you've got around here."

Toni knew she had to get rid of him once and for all. "Hold it. For the *last* time, April and I won the lottery. We didn't know anything about your crummy bearer bonds. And I can prove it."

"Oh yeah? Well, let's hear it, little lady."

"April and I haven't unpacked everything we brought from D.C. yet. We're keeping some boxes in a storage warehouse not too far from here. That's where you'll find the book you stashed your bonds in."

"Ahh, now you're talking. Put some clothes on. Let's go. I'll drive."

Toni dressed quickly, not trusting him out in the living room alone. She was sure he was busy stuffing more of her belongings in his pockets.

No matter. If she had anything to say about it, JB would be back in jail by bedtime. She and April did have a storage shed for some of their furniture that didn't fit into the condo. She planned to get JB inside and lock the door behind him. He'd be safe there until the police arrived.

Toni came out of the bedroom pumped full of adrenaline. "Come on, let's get this over with."

JB rose from the sofa, munching on a fried chicken leg he'd stolen from her refrigerator. "Let's roll. And just in case you don't think I came prepared, I want you to know I have a gun on me. So no sudden moves, yelling, or trying to run. Got it?"

Toni barely swallowed past the tension lodged in her throat. "I got it."

Bolstering her courage, Toni was all set to leave the house and execute her plan to con the con man when the doorbell rang.

"Open up, Toni. It's Blue. We need to talk."

CHAPTER SIXTEEN

JB swore savagely from behind her. "Who the hell is that?"

"My boyfriend." She stared at the door, which was rumbling under Blue's forceful knocking. "Who is infamous for his sense of timing," she said under her breath.

It wasn't that she was unhappy to hear from Blue. In fact, if she'd had time to really think about it, she would have been ecstatic. But she'd had the whole JB situation under control, and now anything could happen. With macho male hormones involved, things could get ugly.

"Get rid of him," JB said, backing down the hall toward her bedroom.

Toni went to the door and opened it a crack. "Blue, what are you doing here?"

"Can I come in? I shouldn't have left the way I did earlier. I've been driving around, thinking. I want to talk."

She knew JB was listening, so she tried to warn Blue

with her eyes. "Um, I don't think tonight's a good time. It's late."

"I know you're mad, Toni. Let me explain."

She couldn't resist the wistful look in those liquid blue eyes. When he pushed on the door, she let him edge his way past her.

"Sweetheart, after we made love tonight—"

"Ouch. I'm crushed." JB strolled into the room. "Antoinette, baby, how could you replace me so soon?"

Blue spun around, leveling his gaze at JB. "Let me guess. This is the loser ex-boyfriend I've been hearing so much about lately."

"Hey, hey, big guy. Don't get your panties in a bunch. I'm not here to move in on you. My girl was just about to give me something that belongs to me, and then I'll be on my way."

Blue shook his head. "I'm afraid it's not going to go down that way, my man."

Toni touched Blue's arm. "It's okay. I do just want to give him what he wants and be rid of him, Blue. Don't worry, I can handle everything."

Again Blue shook his head. "What's the point? He won't be able to spend his money from behind bars."

JB pulled his gun out of his waistband. "Well since you put it like that . . ."

Toni knew what was going to follow couldn't be good, and she couldn't stand the thought of Blue getting shot trying to protect her. Reacting on instinct, Toni did the first thing that came to mind.

She clapped her hands.

The room went dark, and Toni hit the ground. She heard scuffling and a few grunts, but luckily no gunshots. A minute later two sharp claps sounded, and the room once again filled with light.

Blue had brought JB down to the floor, and had him subdued in a wrestling hold. "Call the police, Toni. I hate uninvited guests."

After the police collected JB and left, Toni and Blue were alone. She sat beside him on the sofa.

"Are we finally finished with all this drama? Because I'm ready for it to be over. No more stalking, kidnapping or break ins. Enough is enough."

Blue stretched his arm across her shoulders. "I think it's over. That should be the last you hear of JB and his bumbling brothers."

"Amen to that." Toni leaned back, sighing wearily. "So what made you come back? What did you want to tell me?"

"After I left earlier I drove around, thinking about our last conversation. I realized that I shouldn't have walked out on you the way I did."

Toni shook her head. "I can't blame you. Sounds as if you had a lot to think about, yourself."

"I guess it was my turn to panic. I couldn't believe you were finally telling me what I'd been waiting to hear. Part of me was worried that you'd change your mind when you heard the whole story."

She turned to face him, making sure their gazes connected. "That's my fault. I should have trusted you, and I—"

"No." He touched her lips with his fingers. "You learned to trust me when you were ready to. I *was* trying to rush things between us. I kept looking at what Jax and Coco had, and trying to create those things for us."

"Well, if it helps, I think we're both in the same place now."

"Not quite. There are still a few things I need to tell you. I want you to know everything."

"Don't feel obligated. I know you'll tell me whatever you want me to know, when you're ready."

"I'm ready now. As you know, the 'odd jobs' I've held in my past are more involved than I was willing to talk about."

Toni nodded.

"I don't want you to get the wrong idea. I was never involved in anything illegal. The kind of odd jobs I used to do were for the government. Often it was security work. Making sure some*one* or some*thing* got where it needed to go safely. It usually wasn't pretty, and it was always dangerous work."

"I understand," Toni said. "Even when I realized you weren't ready to talk about your past, I knew it couldn't be anything that could change the way I feel about you. If nothing else, seeing you and JB in the same room proved that."

"I don't do that kind of security work anymore, but as you know I have a lot of friends. People I've met all over the world. Sometimes when they get into a jam, they call me. Lately, I find myself picking up at a moment's notice to go help someone out. That's basically how I got involved with Jax's bodyguard gig last summer."

Toni reached out to take his hand in hers. "Blue, I think it's wonderful that you're so loyal to your friends. I wouldn't have it any other way. I'll never forget what you did for April and me."

"Thanks, but there's one more thing I need you to understand. What you see isn't necessarily what you get. I've seen a lot of things in my lifetime that I'd give anything to forget. Sometimes I can forget. Spending time with you has helped a lot, but it's not always possible for me to block those memories out. I hope you understand that things might get difficult sometimes.''

"Blue, you don't have to hide that side of your personality from me. I want to get to know all of you, and share everything. That takes time, but I'm willing to work on it. Are you?"

"Absolutely."

Their conversation was put on hold when April let herself into the house. "Hey, guys. What's up?"

"April," Toni said. "It's one o'clock in the morning. I figured you were going to stay with Marcus."

"Come on, Toni. We're engaged now. Marcus and I decided to save ourselves for the wedding."

Toni and Blue exchanged looks, unable to hold back their laughter.

April wasn't the least bit bothered. "Don't mind me. I'm just going to make myself some tea and go to bed," she said, disappearing into the kitchen.

Toni looked at Blue. "It is pretty late. Is everything settled between us now?"

Blue nodded. "I think if we agree to be honest with each other, we'll be fine. From now on, we talk about everything."

She smiled at him. "Sounds like a plan to me. Oh, and that reminds me. Get this, JB had hidden bearer bonds inside the jacket of one of the books on my shelf. He had no idea that I'd given all my self-help relationship books to The Salvation Army. Can you believe that? Someone is going to get a big surprise when they open that box of books I sent."

April came out of the kitchen carrying a cup of tea. "Excuse me for interrupting, but I couldn't help overhearing what you guys were saying about honesty and talking about everything, which brings me to a little confession I have to make.''

Toni's eyebrows shot up. "Confession? About what?"

April walked across the room and perched on the arm of the sofa. "Remember that book you lent me several months ago? The one called *No More One-Night Stands?*"

"Yes. I'm still convinced you never read it. Although, now that you and Marcus are together . . ."

"Remember when I said I picked up a few things from it?"

Toni's heart began to hammer in her chest. "Yes."

"Well, here's the confession. We didn't actually win the lottery. I found the bearer bonds in the book, and since Jordan had just gone to jail for miscellaneous cons I kind of put two and two together. I figured he wouldn't be able to spend the money, and it would be poetic justice if you were able to build a new life with it.''

Toni just sat there, with her mouth hanging open.

Blue spoke up. "Wait a minute. This doesn't quite make sense." He turned to Toni. "Didn't you see the lottery ticket when she gave it to you for your birthday?"

"Yes, I did. One day April showed up at my apartment, said we won, and asked for the ticket. She said that since she actually made the purchase, it would be easier if she handled all the paperwork. Next time I saw her, she had the money.''

April shrugged, sipping her tea. "You're not mad, are you? I mean, why not pull a con on the con artist? He was a loser and a jerk. He didn't deserve to have his money back.''

Toni blinked, still trying to take it all in. "That's true.''

Blue shook his head. "I hate to break this to you,

ladies, but if JB is a known con artist, nine chances out
of ten are he didn't come by those bonds honestly. They
probably belong to someone else."

Toni instantly brightened. "Actually that's not true.
While he was here, he mentioned—"

"Wait a minute," April interrupted. "What do you
mean, 'while he was here?' "

"Oh yeah, did I forget to mention that JB broke in
tonight and demanded that I give him his bonds or
make up the difference with our money?"

April glared at her. "No, you didn't mention that.
What happened?"

"Blue showed up, there was a scuffle, and he's in jail
again. I'll explain in detail later. The point is that while
he was here he mentioned that those bonds were proba-
bly the only money that he actually had a right to. The
bearer bonds were an inadvertent gift from his dead
uncle."

Blue threw up his hands. "Then it sounds as if you're
free and clear to me. How do you feel about your ex-
boyfriend financing your new business?"

Toni shrugged. "I say it's the least he could do."

April slumped in relief. "My sentiments, exactly."

Toni caught her sister's eye. "Don't get me wrong.
You and I are going to have a long talk tomorrow, baby
sister. You should have told me the truth."

April yawned, standing up. "It's past my bedtime.
Goodnight, you two."

Toni stood and walked Blue to the door. "It's been
a long night. Will I see you tomorrow?"

He pulled her into his arms. "Absolutely. We have
to start making moving plans. You know how much I
love you, don't you?"

"Yes," she said, snuggling into his embrace. "Just
about as much as I love you." She pulled back and

looked up into his hypnotizing blue eyes. "By the way, I have a pickup line for *you.*"

"Okay, let's hear it."

"What are you doing for the rest of your life?"

Blue leaned down and kissed her gently. "If I'm lucky, I'm spending it with you."

After graduating from college with a degree in psychology, Robyn Amos discovered that writing about the suspenseful and romantic lives of the people in her imagination was more fulfilling than writing scholarly research papers. She sold her first two novels to the Arabesque line soon after joining Washington Romance Writers. Since then she has made a total of six sales. Robyn continues to write about characters from a variety of cultural backgrounds, hoping her stories of romance and adventure will transcend racial stereotypes.

Robyn would love to hear from readers:

P.O. Box 7904
Gaithersburg, MD 20898-7904
Robyn Amos@aol.com

COMING IN MARCH . . .

OPPOSITES ATTRACT   (1-58314-004-2, $4.99/$6.50)
by Shirley Hailstock
Nefertiti Kincaid had worked hard to reach the top at her company. But
a corporate merger may change all that. Averal Ballantine is the savvy
consultant hired to ensure a smooth transition. Feeling as though he is
part of the threat to her career, she hates him sight unseen. Averal will
convince her he's not out to hurt her, but has *all* her best interests in mind.

STILL IN LOVE   (1-58314-005-0, $4.99/$6.50)
by Francine Craft
High school sweethearts Raine Gibson and Jordan Clymer pledged to love
each other forever. But for fear he would be a burden to Raine, Jordan
walked out of her life when he learned he had a debilitating medical
condition. Years later, Jordan returns for a second chance. In the midst
of rekindled passion, they must forge a new trust.

PARADISE   (1-58314-006-9, $4.99/$6.50)
by Courtni Wright
History teacher Ashley Stephens ventures to Cairo, following her love for
archaeology, hoping to escape her boring, uneventful life and enter an
adventure. With her mysterious guide, Kasim Sadam, she is sure to get
her money's worth . . . and a little something extra.

FOREVER ALWAYS   (1-58314-007-7, $4.99/$6.50)
by Jacquelin Thomas
Carrie McNichols is leaving her past to be the best mom to her son. A
lucrative job in L.A. offers her the chance to start over, but she runs into
someone from the past. FBI agent Ray Ransom is her new neighbor and
her old lover. He can't believe fate has given him a second chance. Now
he will do all in his power to protect their love . . . and her life.

Available wherever paperbacks are sold, or order direct from the Pub-
lisher. Send cover price plus 50¢ per copy for mailing and handling to
BET Books, Arabesque Consumer Orders, or call (toll free) 888-345-
BOOK, to place your order using Mastercard or Visa. Residents of New
York, Washington, D.C. and Tennessee must include sales tax. DO
NOT SEND CASH.

LOOK FOR THESE ARABESQUE ROMANCES